WHAT GOES AROUND COMES AROUND

So Keep It 100%

JOSHUA LEVI BROWN

Order this book online at www.trafford.com
or email orders@trafford.com

Most Trafford titles are also available at major online book retailers.

Printed in the United States of America.

ISBN: 978-1-4669-6806-6 (sc)
ISBN: 978-1-4669-6808-0 (hc)
ISBN: 978-1-4669-6807-3 (e)

Library of Congress Control Number: 2012921215

Trafford rev. 03/04/2013

 www.trafford.com

North America & international
toll-free: 1 888 232 4444 (USA & Canada)
phone: 250 383 6864 ♦ fax: 812 355 4082

CONTENTS

PREFACE

All of the names and other identifying characters of the people included in this book are totally fictional and purely coincidental, not intentionally talking about anyone I really know or heard about.

The actual events are totally "play-play," and not real life. Any resemblance to actual persons, living or dead, crimes, places or activities are one-hundred percent, strait coincidental.

Enjoy the ride, baby!

MY DEDICATION

Heaven and Hell

Some things are from Heaven,
Some things are from Hell.
Some things are meant for bad,
Some things are meant to do you well.
Some people are meant to make you stumble,
Some people are meant to make you rise.
Some things are meant to make you dumb,
Some things are meant to make you wise.
Some situations occur to make you stronger,
Some situations occur to make you a fool.
Some situations occur to make you angry,
Some situations occur to make you cool.
Some things happen to test your faith,
Some things happen to test your love.
Some things are truly from the bottom,
Some things are truly from above.
At the end of the night,
At the end of the day,
Realize who is by your side for a moment,
Realize who is by your side to stay.
I thank God that he showed me real love,
All good things are from God above! ☺

I dedicate this to my mom, Evangelist Hannah Sheppard, who paid to have my first two books published, while I was in prison, without me even knowing! Fire in My Soul, and my second book, Real Life Action. I didn't even know I could write!

Thanks so much for Erica Bailey, who met me on Facebook, and wasn't sure if I was a real life person! LOL. Then, she inspired this fun, action-packed story from our conversation! To top it off, Erica typed three books for me, and created the cover design! And this was her first time typing a book or creating a book cover!

I dedicate this to my family, and my kids-Destiny, Saniya, Asia, Yae, and Shay!

This story is for the saved and unsaved. Some good words. Some bad words, 'cause real life is good and bad. But in the end, the fact of life is, What Goes Around, Always Comes Back Around On You!

Thank God for my family and Facebook friends! Enjoy!
11/19/2012

ACKNOWLEDGEMENTS

First, I thank God for giving me a new, unique, different writing swagg and style. God gave me my own writing swagg. Because of God, I'm a swagg author with comedy, inspiration, realness, action, suspense, fantasy and love.

Next, I have to thank my mom, Hannah Sheppard. She turned my first poem into a poetry contest, in Washington, D.C., without me even knowing. Then, it got published and won awards. She also got fifty of my poems published in various books, a book in London, and online at www.poetry.com. Then, she published two more of my books, all while I was in prison, including my Trafford published, best-seller, autobiography called, <u>Real Life Action</u>, which can also be found at amazon.com, and on the Kindle E-book.

Now, I have to thank Erica Bailey, from Saint Louis, to Decatur, Illinois, who I met on Facebook. We instantly became friends. Bam! Surprise. She gave me an idea about this book. I asked her if she could type a book. She typed the entire book before we ever met. Then, she did the book cover with no experience! She typed her first book, and created her first book cover for the first time in her life. So, I must thank Erica. She was in Illinois doing this, while I was in Georgia.

Next, I'd like to thank Porsche Ford for being on my book cover, without initially knowing she would be. LOL,

Thanks to my sister, Kenya Boyd, who always motivates and congratulates me. Also, Kenya created the Kenya PimpCity Brown Facebook fan page, to help promote my book.

I'd like to thank the first people who bought my book, <u>Real Life Action</u>, Cheetara Smith, who also helped me write my first children's book when I helped her daughter with a story over the phone!

Daja Preston, my big sale in Seattle, Washington, and close friend.

Pop AKA Lawrence Rutherford, my good friend and cousin who always support me, and also has a book coming out.

To Erica Bailey's mom, Joyce Brown, a super reader; her kids Arianna, Tianna, Carnell, and Kejuan, and Bre'shauna, her singing, reading daughter.

To Jackie Moultrie, TBN prayer partner, from Griffin, GA. Miss Jackie is seventy-five years old, and read my book with super excitement! She said, "Boy! I thought I was living inside your book! I love it so much! I read it twice! Ready for your next one!"

Tamala Combs, one of my first sales up in Tennessee. Much love to you, your kids, and your sister. Thanks to Dee Mccounly in Cobb County. Shout out to Kishana Pettis. Cedar Grove High School popular, pretty star.

Mr. Reynolds and Miss Walker, much love.

Mizz Tye Daniel, aka Tyeshia Daniel, the Columbia High School, East Atlanta, singing sensation, with one of those special, superb, singing voices, and the hardest underground CDs ever to touch the streets! One of the best voices you could ever hear.

Thanks to TBN worker, mom's great friend, wonderful author, Reverend Frieda (Fritz) Porter, author of <u>On the Brink of the Rapture.</u>

Cedra Glover, for always having my back. Danika Holloway, for having my back, buying thirty copies of <u>Real Life Action</u>, and having her son to write a report on it! Much love Feetie, Erica, Catedra, Africa, Keisha, Shon, Aunty Van, Shaneia, Saniya and the twins. Shout out to Michael Lackey, aka White Mike, the Cobb County representer.

To Lexie. Lexie, wow, fourteen years old, and she read <u>Real Life Action</u> in less than a day! Nonstop! Her mom and granddad had to make her put my book down on Thanksgiving Day to eat! Lexie ate the turkey and read the book at the same dang time! Much love, Dontae, my godson. Everybody, including his mom, Porsche, tried to get him to read. He picked up my book, <u>Real Life Action</u>, and it was his first time reading a book! He knocked it out, and been reading ever since then!

Much love to Rachael Moore at TBN T.V. station for always supporting me and helping with my first book. Miss Lizz. Every time she bought a copy of my book, <u>Real Life Action</u>, she would show it to somebody. They would say, "Wow. This is bad!" then keep it! Lizz would smile, and buy another copy! She bought twenty copies of <u>Real Life Action</u>! So, Atlanta knows me well! LOL. Love you, Lizzie, A.K.A. Liz Ward.

Thanks to Miss Milsap and her daughter Mercia for the strong support for me. Plus, for helping me with my first book.

Kenyatta Joiner, special shout out. The youngest person to buy my book. Chicago born and always got my back. Too cool, funny, but serious at the same dang time. Much love.

Tanisha Moncure, my first Chicago fan who just loved my book so much. Showed me so much love and support. Thanks.

To Ivory Grant, Debra Grant, and family. Special thanks for supporting me in Illinois! Ivory said that book is fire!

My homie, Chalay, Dogman, Hood, Ciarea, Supreme and Ladonna. Momma Regina, and Tremya. Mastajjea Grimes. Much love. Muslims, Mob, Bloods, Crips, Gangstas, Murk Squad.

To Iesha Honeycutt, showing me love all the way in Alaska! Thanks! First Alaska sale.

Onlyone Aae Enuffsaid, my Tampa, Florida supporter! Always encouraged me! Bought my book, and I only know her Facebook name! LOL.

Stozzi Grimes, sings so good. Keep pushing CD's in Illinois and ATL. Thanks for supporting my books!

Courtney Smith, thanks for the love. Columbia High on Columbia Dr. in Decatur, GA. Much love!

Dajanae Hawkins, Janise Freeman, Crystal and Diamond. Special shout out!

Amanda Young and Dustin Reece. Scott and D.J. Mac. My great, Detroit friend-Kenya Taliferro. Super cool. Detroit in the house!

Lil sister Devin Porter, Kim Harris, Deonna Harris, my sis. Tatiana and Fat Daddy, Yae Allen, my kool daughter. Shay Carter, the flyest daughter in the world.

Destiny, my first born, pretty angel with swagg and talent. Saniya, my beautiful, reading seven year old, story-teller and singing daughter/

want to be famous author, like her daddy! Asia, my pretty, six year old, rap star, swagg daughter. Lisa Daniels, my friend, forever. My Uncle Douglas Rozier. Love you. Champ, J.B., Nicole and Jameka Mackey, my best friend. Adela and Tiffani, Dreauna Houston, my Las Vegas friend. Jessica Speed, Jasmine Mackey, my inspirational, navy, little sister. Keep up the good military work. Erica Brown.

Aajanique Long, the cover girl. Clarence, Buster, Ron, Micki Pettis, Shannisha Thomas, Ciera More, my mom's good friend and young model Shay A.K.A. Nashanta LaShay Brown. Esomin Amador, my good, cool friend. Brittany Backley, super Griffin singer. Myah Godlock, for the surprise support of my book. Danie Bailey, my cool, Jamaican sister, who is also an author. I love you. Cyera Allbritton, Shanda Pope, Erika Brown in Minnesota. Ashley Pope, Shirley Jones.

Jalisa Smith, my good friend. April Mayfield, Sharonda Cherry, Keith Cooper, Alisha Elliot, Charlotte Taylor, my first supporter in Texas. Tyeshia Evans, for always showing love. Nu-Nu, Lexie, Dontae, Layla and Malik. Nu-Nu, keep doing good. Porsche's friend, Diamond. Crystal Weaver, East Atlanta model. Princess Akins and all my thousands of FB friends! Cierra Holmes, Kalisa Seaborough.

To my best friend and homie, Trap. To Danielle Cheeks. My uncle Alonzo Grant. Nicole Johnson. Chanda Wise and kids. Erica and the Wise family. Raven, my beautiful, singing niece. Tricia Butterball and family in Griffin. Love you Tricia. My cousin, Lakesia Moreland, love you up in Brooklyn, New York! Singing Veronica in Carolina! My brother, Danny Lyons, A.K.A. Baldhead. My brothers Brandon Bonner, Lou and Usef.

Special thanks to my three brothers and sister, who I just I just met last year. Cimeon, Sergio, Deon, and lil' sister Shawn Riley. We all got the same dad-Earl Brown and he a pure Jamaican! Wooh!

Thank Everyone. Much love!

FOREWORD

If someone were to give you this book without revealing the author's identity, you would never believe that the author is male. I have yet to find a male author, who has solely (not co-written) a book quite like this one-from a woman's point of view. Then I met Joshua Levi Brown, and as I was typing this book for him, I had to keep reminding myself that I didn't write the book; he did! LOL.

Allow me to introduce myself. My name is Erica Bailey. I met Joshua on Facebook, not realizing that I had just met the "Tyler Perry of the book world!" Not actually knowing who he was, and not yet meeting him in Real Life, I wasn't sure if he was even a real person, or a real author, until I did my research. Then I was amazed because despite his circumstances, he still had quite an ability to "interact with people" and promote one of his first books, <u>Real Life Action</u>, online! LOL. Anyways, like the majority of people who encounter this man, we instantly became friends, and our conversations led to the development of this book. Somehow, I ended up creating the book cover, typing this book, and two more books by this unforgettable author.

Why me? Who am I, and why would I do what I've done for a total stranger? Well, a lot of people tend to judge a person because of their past or where they come from. And still, others will hate on you because you have talent, and are trying to make it in this world. Me? I'm the total opposite. I always try my hardest to think positive and give people the benefit of the doubt, no matter what they may have done in their past. Anything positive you're trying to do to make a better life for you and your family, hey, I'm down. It's NEVER too late. Keep doing what you do, Josh. You are SO talented. You and your writing . . . YOU SHOULD HAVE BEEN RICH!!!!

Joshua had written yet another entertaining, best-seller. <u>What Goes Around, Comes Around, So Keep It 100%</u> is an action-packed book that many people can relate to. The readers become the characters, feeling how they feel, thinking what they think. As you read, so many emotions will travel through your head and heart, as they did mine, while I was typing this book. You will feel like you're there, in every setting, every club, at every house and in every car, while Joshua takes you along for this ride. One minute you'll feel desperate and heart-broken, like you can't go on. The next minute, you're thankful to be alive!

The main character in this book, Erica Brown has been through it all. No one is perfect, but no one deserves to be treated like she is. Beatings, cheating, lying, crying, heartache, and deceit, her man takes her through it all! Like Erica, we all go through situations in our lives, and some of them have us thinking to ourselves, *Why me? Why is this happening to me? What did I do that was so wrong? What did I do to deserve this?* The next thing you know, you're reading the paper or watching the news, and hearing stories about massive killings, illness, catastrophe, child abuse, deadly storms . . . that's when you start to realize that your life is not so bad, compared to some.

That is what this book teaches. It reminds readers that there is always someone who's in a situation ten times worse than yours. People will do you wrong, and you will want to seek revenge. Let go, and let God. Talk about it, cry about it, pray about it, learn from it, and get over it, because what goes around, comes around. Instead, look forward to what the future holds and what God has in store for you, despite what hell you've been through in the past, and what madness is going on in the present.

Like his first book, <u>Real Life Action</u>, <u>What Goes Around, Comes Around, So Keep It 100%</u> will have your heart racing, anticipating what comes next. I won't reveal too much, but there are several parts in this book where I wanted to skip ahead just to see what happened! Joshua has a way with words (and sound effects ☺). He can touch his readers like no other author can. I remember reading a part of the book that gave me goose bumps as I was typing. Erica Brown was in a life or death situation. She felt hopeless, and at one time, she contemplated suicide. Joshua writes:

I seriously considered suicide! But why live in hell, then die, and go to hell?! SUICIDE is Double Hell! If I kill myself, that's the only sin I can't be forgiven for, because I'll already be dead, and can't pray!

I had to STOP TYPING! I was thinking to myself *WOW! Now that was deep! I've never looked at it like that.*

If you have read <u>Real Life Action,</u> you know that Joshua has been in some INSANE situations! Only by the grace of God is he still here! I've told him, "you and God have to be best friends!" LOL. But though it all, he is still such an outgoing and positive person, and continues to change his life for the better.

Categorizing <u>What Goes Around, Comes Around, So Keep It 100%</u> for the publishing company was kind of hard, because you can place this book in so many categories of writing. Do we place this book in the category of

A. Family and Relationships? Yea.
B. Fictional/Action and Adventure? Oh, yea!
C. Humor/General? Yes.
D. Religion/Inspirational? Yes.
E. Self-Help/General? Sure ☺

No one word can describe Joshua's style of writing. It's comical, mind-blowing, deep, action-packed, knowledgeable, and heart-breaking all at the same time. So, I'll just say Joshua is a FIGHT writer. Funny, Inspirational, Gratifying, Hood, and Thrilling.

<u>What Goes Around, Comes Around, So Keep It 100%</u> emphasizes that at the end of the day, when it's all said and done, it doesn't matter who you are. When you do wrong, WRONG WILL DO YOU! Karma ain't no joke, and God still don't like ugly! What Goes Around, Comes Around, So Keep It 100%

You have purchased a great book! Enjoy!

Erica Bailey
Decatur, IL
January 2013
~Hustle-N-Flow~

Erica Bailey
Reppin' St. Louis, MO and Decatur, IL.
Cover Designer, Editor, actress, clothing designer, and she can sing!

PROLOGUE

"Now, that's the shid I don't like!" Kenya PimpCity Brown rapped, while her and Porsche cruised through the brilliantly lit up city of Atlanta.

"Porsche Two Fine Brown."

"What up, Skinny Smalls?"

"Shid B, just chillin . . ."

POW! BAH! Baw! Boom!

Gunshots; two, three vehicles exploded! The gas station windows shattered. The money green Escalade crashed into pump 10.

KAH-BOOM!!!!

It ignited the entire gas station. People's entire bodies were exploding . . .

God, is this the end of the world? Is the world coming to an end, even in the ghetto?!

"Kenya! Hit reverse! Hit reverse, B! The fire comin' towards us!" Porsche kicked, pointed, and screamed.

"Not!" Kenya PimpCity Brown yelled, appearing to remain as cool as a cigarette in a polar bear's mouth, with knee high boots, wearing a black thong, in the North Pole!

"Dog!" Kenya barked, switching gears in her new, gold and black Benz. She looked in her rearview mirror, and realized she only had nearly three inches of space separating her and the old beat up Honda.

Rrrrrrhhooooom! ZZZZZOOOOOOOM! Boom! Boom!

Screeeeach! Tire rubber burning . . .

She hit the front of the Honda, and quickly slung the Benz into drive.

Instantly, the race began!

The dark smoke was filing the air like deadly fog. She power pushed the gas. The scary smoke was following the ATL Bad Girls like a run-a-way slave in a volcano forest fire!

The cracklin' flames burned everything in sight.

Someone ignited a devastating bomb-right, smack in the middle of the downtown, ATL club scene!

At seven PM, it appeared to be midnight on Mars! Lightless!

Kenya PimpCity Brown turned her head to the sidewalk.

"Move, Bitc . . .!" she yelled at the redbone, on the curb, as she sent her Benz gliding fast on the sidewalk.

Melt! Cheese bologna!

The redbone instantly turned into a burnt bone, when the flames hit her red ass!

"Go! Go! GO!" Porsche yelled, still smoking a blunt of that ghetto Kenya! (Kenya was the new code word for string marijuana).

It was hilarious, how Porsche was yelling and turning back and forth, pointing at the fire clouds that were chasing the Benz. Through all that yelling, wow! Porsche refused to stop or drop that blunt! If she died, she was dying high and fly!

BANG!

"Dang!"

They hit a pole.

Ka-bang! The pole fell on the hood of the car. Crack . . .

"Duck, girl!" Kenya yelled, as the light pole crushed the front seat; smack in the middle of the two ATL bad girls.

"Go! Get out! Run!" Porsche yelled.

"Grab my baby!" Kenya yelled, in horror!

Could they beat the fire; or die?

"Cocaine! Grab auntie's hand!" Porsche screamed, snatching Kenya's one year old son, Cocaine King Brown.

"Coca-Cola! Hold on to mama tight!" Kenya said, grabbing her one year old daughter, out of the platinum car seat.

Coca-Cola Platinum Brown was Cocaine's twin. She had green eyes, and Cocaine had red eyes.

"Ahhh!"

Porsche tripped over a pack of gummy bears. Baby Cocaine went flying in the air.

Swissh!

"Gotcha!" Kenya PimpCity Brown snatched baby Cocaine out of the air.

"Grab my boots!" Kenya shouted.

Porsche grabbed ahold of Kenya's black knee high boots, right before she hit the ground!

The blunt was still in her mouth.

"Here!" Kenya yelled, passing baby Coca-Cola to Porsche.

The girls ran faster than two cheetahs on speed.

However, sadly . . . the girls weren't fast enough to beat the bomb. The fire caught the two pretty girls and the twin babies.

WOOOOF! WHIF!

Chop, chop, chop.

"Grab it!" Daja yelled.

God!

The girls grabbed onto the golden ladder of the black and gold AH-1 Cobra war helicopter. They were rushing, wildly and anxiously, fighting and struggling to climb up the ladder, sweating! I raised the helicopter higher away from the flames and deadly smoke.

Crying . . . Babies hollering . . .

"Come on. Uggh. Pull!" Danika and Daja yelled to each other, at the same dang time. As the two Seattle cuties pulled Kenya, Porsche, and the twins onto the AH-1 Cobra chopper, the first ever war helicopter created on earth.

"Erica Hustle-N-Flow Brown! Dang, girl! You just saved our lives. I owe you for this, baby. Ima always have your back!" Kenya PimpCity Brown told me, as she sat her twins on my leather seats.

"Mizz Tye, don't you got a concert tonight?" Diamond asked the East ATL singer.

"Yea, down there by you in Tampa. But I got to go to Glenwood, and get all the way Turned UP!" Mizz Tye shouted, and we all laughed.

"Nu Nu. Lexie. Who ass yall whuppin' now?" Porsche asked her two pretty fighting dolls.

"Who the hell tried to blow up Atlanta?" Cedra asked on my iPhone.

"Joe Brown," I replied, as I continued to fly my one-hundred and twenty-two thousand dollar helicopter.

"And why in the yellow raincoat, bride of Chucky, hot hell, would Joe Brown blow up ATL?" Kenyatta asked in my ten seater helicopter.

I had a T.V., a PlayStation 10, a couch, and a Jacuzzi in my AH-1 chopper.

"Cause I told you, I was gonna set the city on fire, as soon as I got free!!" Joe Brown bragged, as he relaxed in the gold-plated Fusion Whirlpool Jacuzzi, blowing smoke out of his mouth.

Lord . . . I think I have got the craziest baby daddy in the world! Matter of fact, the craziest baby daddy on Earth and Mars, at the same dang time. LOL.

"Let's ride!" I yelled to my ATL Bad Gurl Crew!

"NIGGA PLEASE!"

'Can I Get a Refill' was playing loud on my phone. I was on my computer, feeling super good because I was about to marry my high school sweetheart. I was six months pregnant with my first baby, a boy!

"Hell naw!" I yelled.

I couldn't believe my eyes! I was on my boyfriend's Facebook page. He was so high, that he forgot to log out! Smoking on that damn Keysha, and cheating with my twin sister, Keysha!

> Joe to Keysha: You got that fye! Last night was great. I wish I woulda met you first! Your butt is bigger too! Damn you got that thunder!

'I never knew love would hurt so bad . . .
Worse pain that I ever had
I never knew love could feel like a heart attack!'

That song was banging in my heart. I held my chest. My heart felt like a wet, wild lion was chewing on it like bubblegum. I took a deep breath, and continued to read.

> Keysha to Joe: Bull shit! You raped me, nigga! You put something in my drink! Plus, I thought you was Jitt! I'm glad you in boxed me, dummy! The police will see the evidence!

Joe to Keysha: LOL, silly wide butt, slut. Shut the liver licking, tongue kissing, dry cat up! You popped that couchie and made it clap! You backed it up, like a Donk! You wasn't drunk! You kangaroo, couchie breath tramp!

Plus, you knew Jitt was with Whitney! You sent them to the stoe, Hoe! Now Miss Keysha, the man pleaser, wood squeezer! If you tell the police, who will raise that innocent, first born baby your sister is having?

Huh? Big Mouth of the South! Your nephew would be without a father! Because of you! Trick! She would raise her son alone! It would be all your fault!

Keysha to Joe Brown: Fuck you!

POW! Hard hitting messages!
I took another breath, and read more crap!

Joe to Micki Redbone Shawty, Sexy Red, are you mixed? I see you are married, you stay in Atlanta, and you are from Augusta. Well, I'm from Bankhead, Shawty. If you ever want a real nigga that keep it 100, holla at me. I will give you a thousand dollars, just for a kiss.

Micki Redbone Shawty to Joe: LOL. Cute, but not cute enuff. My husband gives me twenty-thousand a week boo, just to grocery shop. So take that little weak, west side game, that basketball fade away hair line, and your purple rain face, back to Bankhead! Shawty!

Bam!
I threw the lamp at his head!
"Damn wifey, what's wrong?" Joe asked, like a cross-eyed turkey with thongs.
I was one inch away from painting the wall fruit punch red, with his head!
"Nigga, please! Don't wifey me! You Dog! I can't believe you! You raped my sister, Joe! We supposed to get married next month! I'm pregnant with your son. I can't . . ."

Tears rushed out. I couldn't hold it in. How could this nigga do me like this?!

"Baby," he tried to put his arm around my neck.

"No!" I pushed the dog off me.

Slap! I slapped the pink cow liver piss out of him!

Bam! "Biiiitch!"

"God, Joe! My nose!" I said in pain, holding my nose and falling to the floor. He hit me hard. I heard my nose crack.

Bam! Bam! Kick! Kick! Kick!

The pain was too much. He was kicking me hard with his Polo boots, while I curled up on the floor. Then he picked me up and body slammed me like I was a damn wrestler, instead of the mother of his first child!

"Ah!"

He kicked me in the stomach.

"My baby . . ."

"Damn this baby! You stupid hoe!"

"Hold up nigga, don't hit my sister!"

Bam!

"Nigga, I'll hit you too!" Joe yelled, punching my brother Dontae so hard, he flew back first, into the wall.

"Ima kill you!" Joe yelled in his African tone.

I passed out.

"Yea, I knocked out a brother and a sister, at the same damn time!" Joe bragged, laughing and remixing the Future song.

Then, Joe hopped into his candy apple red Cadillac truck, beating the East Atlanta rapper, Future's remix, 'At the Same Damn Time.'

WHY ME?

Who is that white girl? Where am I? Was I dreaming? Hold up!

"Where is my baby?"

"Calm down, Miss Brown."

"Nooo! Calm down my cat! Where is my baby?!"

I was in an uproar; like a Waka Flocka fan!

"Miss Brown, we couldn't save your baby, the baby died . . ." the young petite nurse said.

Tears began to shoot out of my eyes like pepper spray. My chest started stinging. I was devastated. Hurt. Heartbroken. Lost . . .

The nurse tried to explain, but I couldn't hear one word. Everything was double. All I could think about was that I lost my first child; by the hands of his own father . . .

In the meantime, Joe was headed to Pimp City, the hot, sexy strip club in Decatur, GA.

"What up, China?"

"Hey baby," China said, blushing like a sneaky, happy gold digger.

He hugged her, and squeezed her delicious behind.

"Hey Big Money," the cutest waitress with honey brown skin said. She looked like Lauren London; her name was Vanilla Bean.

"Oh, I'm super good, now that I see you," Joe said with eyeballs bigger than a catfish on crack!

"Hey Mama!" I said, happy as a pig in muddy water.

"Hey Sugar. Are you ok?" my loving mama said.

I loved her! Joyce Brown, my heart and soul. My best friend. I remember when I got jumped on by three little fat girls in kindergarten; mama ran into the school and whipped all three of the fat bad little piggies!

"Baby, how are you?"

"I'm ok, Mama." I lied.

I was far from ok. As far as Mississippi is from China! Man, I felt like I just swallowed a Good Year Tire, licked some puppy ear wax, and sniffed some elephant fart!

Tears forced through my pain. My mama hugged me. I cried on her shoulder, while we held each other tighter than a prisoner hugging his girlfriend during visitation.

Five months later, I was on Facebook, checking out my homeboy page, Joshua ATLShawty Brown. Wow! He kept drama on his wall. Some dark, cute, chick named Jolly Rancher, was having words with Adreana Toocute Jones.

> **Jolly**-"That's my man, trick!"
>
> **Adreana**-"I can't tell! He paid my phone bill and rent at the same damn time!"
>
> **Jolly**-"He bought me a car and a puppy at the same damn time!"
>
> **Keke**-"Yall are some dumb hoes, arguing over a nigga in prison."
>
> **Porsche**-"Naw, my cuzzin is a damn king, and a pimp."
>
> **Kenyatta**-"I'm wifey; I'm in all of his books."
>
> **Kenya**-"Yall girls are too funny. Last time I checked, I was the one he hugged at visitation. And I'm the only one that comes to see him while he's down. Yall are just wild fans!"
>
> **Kenyatt**a-"Oh, really, Miss Pimp City? I will leave Chicago, and come down South, and stick my size 5 in your eyes."
>
> **Kenya**-"I don't argue hun; I know who's the boss."

Booch-"Look, look, yall hoes f . . . with my cousin, and Ima flip yall hoes like dominoes!"

Antwon Jitt-"Yea, my sister ain't gotta argue on nobody's wall. Yall hoes grow up!"

CeeCee-"Damn Josh, you hotter than a Fireball, on the 4ᵗʰ of July, in a Dragon's mouth!"

Kenya-"Whatever. One word for yall thirsty hoes, BOOP!"

Daja-"Wow"

Cheetara-"LOL"

Danie-"Kill the drama with my brother."

I loved Facebook! It was too funny. People believe Facebook, like it's the Holy Bible!

"Erica, I love you."

"Huh?"

"Give daddy a kiss," Joe said in his African, jungle love tone.

Oh, he had been gone for five months! Probably busting more nuts than a squirrel!

"I miss you, Erica!"

"Oh, Really?!" I yelled, hugging him like a bear on drugs.

I know I should have pushed him away. Joe was fine though! 6 foot even. Brown as dirt on the smooth ground. Perfect skin; like a baby's booty! Pretty boy, baby face. Deep ocean, play boy waves. Tattoos everywhere. Chest was prison fine; hard as a rock! Sexy as Chris Brown with a body like The Rock! Amen Mary J! I love my Mr. Wrong too!

"Move! You crazy, nasty, bulldog licking nigga!"

"What, baby?" Joe said, playing innocent.

"Nigga!"

Slap! Slap!

"Wait!" Joe grabbed my arm out the air, like a center fielder in baseball!

"Why you slapping me?"

"Cause! Your neck, Joe! You African bootey scratcher!"

"Oh, my mom sucked my neck on accident when . . ."

Bam!

I punched the lie outta his mouth!

"Now, I'm bout to kill you!" Joe yelled, grabbing my neck, like a basketball.

"No you ain't gonna kill my baby; nor even touch my daughter."

"Oh, I'm sorry, Miss Brown," Joe told my mom. He looked like a little kid getting caught by a Sunday School teacher, for stealing peppermint out of a purse in church!

"Ok, you African, tiger boy. Don't make momma whip you with a vine from the jungle, and throw your wanna be ATL West-side American butt back on the banana boat!"

"Ha, ha, Momma you silly." I laughed snot out my nose.

"Not playing baby. Joe, I'm serious as a lion in the jungle. Touch my daughter and die, boy."

"Yes mam," Joe said, walking outside to his new car, with his head down.

"Got Dam of Sam!" I was shocked.

"What now, Erica?"

"That car! Shitty, whitty! How on poppa smurf hell did you get that?!"

Joe laughed out loud.

"The game been good, even in the hood. Get in."

I got in, after he opened to door like a gentleman. I was stunned! He was driving one of those Maybach things. You know, the kind of car I've only seen in those Rick Ross videos!

We sat in the car. It had black fur seats with a real leopard floor. The interior was Pimp My Ride Smooth.

"Joe, we can't live like this forever. I'm going back to school. Do you plan on selling drugs forever?"

"Naw, I rob too, sometimes," he laughed.

"Shut up, Joe. Street life, leads to prison life. Fast money goes fast."

"So what? You only live once, so ball till you fall."

Boom! Boom! Pow!

Gun shots. My chest. Blood, dang. I held my chest.

"What the? You shot? You ok?"

I shook my head. "Yea, I guess."

"Good cause somebody got to die!" Joe jumped out the candy apple red, rap video car.

Two Dred headed teenagers were arguing with a huge, fat guy. His name was Big Butler Bun.

"Yall F . . . . niggas shot my car!"

"Man, F . . . yo car!"

Pow! Pow! Pow! Joe shot all three of them, at the same dang time!

Then, this jungle, arrow shooting idiot jumped in the car, like he ain't did a green gummy bear thang!

"Joe, baby, this ain't Africa. You ain't in the jungle!"

"Ha, ha. Americans are weak. Yall got white man's blood."

"Joe, you got dumb dumb blood. We have court rooms in America!" He laughed.

"Hello?"

"What's up baby girl?" my uncle O.G. Hood said. He was calling me from prison.

"Oh, I got the Green Dot."

"Thank you, baby girl. How much is it? I gotta smoke."

"It's a hundred."

"Fo sho! Text the numbers."

"Hey, tell Dog Man and Green, Ima shoot them a hundred today."

"Bet," uncle Hood replied.

Then, I texted my uncle the fourteen numbers that I scratched off the Green Dot Money Pack card, I purchased from Walgreens.

We were quiet as we rode to his third house in College Park.

"What is this, Joe?"

"Oh, that's my sister," he lied.

"Joe, I can read. Who the hell is Kaylin?"

"That's Daja. You know I had to switch my sister name."

"Why?"

"So the police won't know. I got you saved as Nicki Minaj in my phone."

"You silly. You're a quick liar, but not a good one. Daja is in Seattle. Why would Atlanta police want her? She works. Look, just stop lying. I wish you would change. I love you, Joe. I want a family with you. You are my first love."

I'M ON FIRE!

The rapper, Lil Boosie, blasted loud from the Maybach.

"Joe, when are you gonna stop selling drugs?"

"Erica, when are you gonna stop being a female?"

Wap!

I hit him on the shoulder. We both laughed.

"Seriously, Joe. I'm a pretty girl. I don't want fifteen black eyes a month, and ten broke noses a year. I want to be loved."

I stared at the side of his face, while I talked. He continued to look forward.

"Erica, can we change the past, or the present?"

"Joe, our baby woulda been two months."

"Oh well, what the hell. Guess we gotta work on another one!" he laughed.

"Too late. I'm five weeks pregnant."

Scccccreeeach! The tires yelled, the breaks started roaring.

"By who? Bruce Leroy?!"

"Ha, ha. Who else, idiot? You!"

Bang!

The nigga crashed into a tree, destroying the new car. Now, it looked like a broken pencil!

"See what you made me do!"

"Nigga Please!" I just rolled my eyes, while the engine smoked.

Flames started sparking up. The car was instantly blazing with fire. I was stuck! My eyes were glued to the flames. I couldn't breathe. Joe was trying to kick out the windshield.

"Hold on, baby. We ain't gonna die like this!"

I heard him, but I was losing air.

Bang! Boom!

He pulled me out, after he kicked the door off.

What the hell? The Lil Wayne song was blasting from the Fire truck- 'The Fire Man.'

Yeah, I had to be dreaming. But my all white Polo Outfit was as black as a burnt Tom and Jerry cartoon!

I had twisted my ankle, so I was stuck in the house, blowing up Joe's phone. Finally, after the thirty-fifth call, a female answered.

"Will you please stop calling Joe?"

"What?! Who the hell are you?!"

"Hmm. I'm his girlfriend, Precious."

"Hmm, and I'm about to kick your Precious Ass!"

"Really, sweetie? And where are you, cause I'm with him."

"Yeah, yeah, yeah. Meet me somewhere!"

"Ok, meet me at the Holiday Inn, and bring a friend, cause he licking on me, and ready to spend."

"Which one?"

"Down town, Miss Brown," the trick said.

"Yeah, let me see you rhyme, when I beat you to death!"

I limped out of the house, and knocked on my next door neighbor's door.

Knock, knock, knock.

I stood at her door in my too tight, short, Polo sweat pants.

"What's up, girl?"

"Kenya, I need a ride," I said, unable to hold back.

"What's up? Do I smell a fight?" Kenya asked.

"Naw, you smell a hotel beat down!" I yelled.

"I want in!" Joe's sister Daja said, from out of nowhere.

"Let's ride! Kenya Pimp City Brown, and Erica Hustle-N-Flow Brown, bout to beat a slut down to the ground!" Kenya said. She was my neighbor, and my friend. She was beautiful; mixed with black and white.

She looked like a young Mariah Carey. Right now, I looked like a more chocolate Nicki Minaj, with a red Atlanta Braves miniature baseball bat in my hand. We listened to dat song, 'Ima beat that p . . . . up, up, up, up, up.'

We got downtown in seven minutes. I dialed Joe's number. Damn! She a bold slut.

"Bout time you showed up, hoe. I'm in room 112!"

Me and the girls flew up the steps.

Gunshots! We froze. The door to 112 swung open.

"What? Yall hoes thought it would be a fair fight?" Precious said.

Pow!

Damn! She shot the girl!

Precious dropped like a brick.

"Ahh!" Precious cried, holding her leg.

Kenya PimpCity Brown, shot her ass down! She had pulled out her pink .22, from her pink Polo boot.

"Don't cry now!"

Me, Daja, and Kenya stomped her until the cops came.

"Lock these stupid hoes up." Joe said, standing with the two tall cops. The cop named Butler, slung Kenya down, scratching her face. He was at least four-hundred pounds, on a light day. He rammed his large knees into her back.

"Help! Man, that hurt!"

"Shut up," Officer Butler yelled. The other two officers slung me face first into the door, instantly making my nose bleed.

The other white cop tried to grab Joe's sister, Daja.

"Get back! I'll cut your throat!" Daja warned, pulling out a sharp box cutter.

Then a female officer grabbed Kenya.

"Punk!" she yelled, spitting in the cop's face.

"Drop your weapon, or I'll shoot," the female officer said, aiming at Daja's head.

Pow! Pow!

I couldn't believe it. Everybody froze.

The big officer Butler, and the female officer, Walker, shot Joe's sister twice!

"No! No! No!" Joe went crazy. He started punching the cops.

They left me, without handcuffs on. All the attention was on Joe, so Kenya and I ran to the car. Her wrists were so small, she slid out of the hand cuffs. We jumped into her money green Cadillac truck and sped off.

"Kenya, turn that down girl!" I told my friend. She loved playing her music loud. Boosie and Future were her favorite.

My mom was calling.

"Hello?"

"Baby, you saw the news? That child got shot!"

"Who?"

"The African's sister."

"Daja?"

"Yeah. It's all on the news girl! Your man went junglenuts!" my mom said, laughing. She swore all Africans were bad. However, I loved my King Kong.

"Is she alive?" I asked with concern.

"Don't know sweetie. She in critical condition. The news showing Joe, fighting like a wild lion!"

"Ha, ha."

"Shut up girl. Jungle Love." my mom joked.

"Love you, Mom."

"Love u too, child."

I jumped out of Kenya's car, and went into the house. I turned on the news. Rachael was explaining the incident.

"Channel 5 news, live at the Holiday Inn, in Downtown Atlanta. We have breaking news about the police shooting of twenty-one year old Daja Presly from Seattle. She was not the only victim. Eighteen year old Precious McCledon was also shot. By whom, we have yet to discover. Precious was apparently beaten very badly. She had ten teeth missing, a broken nose, and her ear was cut off with a box cutter. The moment we find out more, we will inform you."

I laughed, hella hard. Then I changed the channel to a video by Alicia Keys. I closed my eyes, thinking about how we beat that girl. I broke her nose, while we were stomping her. Kenya pistol whipped her and knocked out ten teeth. Daja broke her jaw with my bat. I cut her ear off with Kenya's box cutter; all this over a no good nigga! We shoulda been whippin' his ass!

JAIL BIRDS DON'T FLY, BUT THIS ONE DID!

So, my man had been in Fulton County Jail for four hours. He was already blowing my phone up.

"Erica, where you at?"

"Joe, I'm leaving momma's house."

"Who you been sleepin' wit'? Who you been fuckin?"

"Nobody, Joe! "Who the hell is Mungie?"

"Oh that's Jitt girl."

"Well why in the corndog hell would Jitt girl be sending you picture messages of her putty cat?"

"Cause his phone got wet."

"Well, yo ass about to get wet, cause I ain't getting you out, nigga. Big Bubba bout to get that booty!"

I laughed hard. He didn't. I could feel this nigga's heated anger. He was Incredible Hulk mad! Joe had a probation hold, so they wouldn't let him out. I stood by his side like a real Ride or Die chick!

I was driving my new candy apple red Honda with my brand new pedicure twenty inch gold rims. I was talking to my man, collect from the jail.

"Why is this white man following me?"

"What?! Is he a police?" Joe asked, from the prison phone.

"Huh? Naw. He's driving next to me. He wants my number."

"What?! Don't disrespect me!"

"He must like me. Ima give him a shot Joe," I joked.

"Yeah, and Ima give both of yall a shot of lead!" Joe barked, like a pet bull dog, named Cupcake!

I stopped at the red light.

"Joe, I'm joking. He could be a serial killer anyway. Too nice looking, innocent and happy. The perfect serial killer type."

"Yea well, all white men ain't serial killers, and all Africans ain't from the jungle!"

"Heellllp!"

"Baby? Baby?"

I dropped the phone. The guy had a knife to my neck! He tried to open the passenger door.

"Time to get raped!" he laughed like a devil.

I was terrified. I'd never been raped before. He had his hands through my window; the knife on my throat. Why did I even stop for a stranger? There wasn't another car in site.

Bam!

"Ouch."

Santanna knocked him out!

"What the hell was the nerdy white dude doin' in your car with a knife?"

"Tryna rape me, San."

San was my cousin. He was in an organized crime family, started in Atlanta, called the MOB, and the other group was called the Good Fellas, or YMF.

"Well, the only thing he will be raping is the ground, lil cousin. I just did twelve hard years in the Georgia Prison System, and if anybody touch my family, I'll go right back with no problem. I'm a real ATL O.G. MOB shit for life!"

"Aww, thank you. I love you, cuz. You so hard." I told my cousin, hugging his neck.

"What up nigga? What's poppin?" San asked Joe.

"Man, is she alright? Did the white man rape her?"

"No, Joe." San responded.

"Where you living, shawty?"

"My nigga, I'm moving to Colorado."

"Damn! Watch out for those pretty white girls!" Joe said, laughing.

"Get the phone cuz, I'm out. I don't want to bust your man up!"

I pushed my cousin's arm and we both laughed.

"Here cuz, I love you. I'm about to leave the ATL, and see other parts of the world. You are my favorite little cousin. What I want you to do, is live your life. Love yourself and God, and complete all your goals. I love you. Here, this is my gift to you."

"Dog! Dog! Puppy fart! San! Wow! Thank you cuz! I love you!" I shouted.

I was so happy, I had tears in my eyes. My cousin gave me twenty-thousand dollars, and a platinum necklace with Erica on the charm. My name was silver and gold with diamonds in it.

We hugged, and I smiled like a baby, as San drove off in his new red and black 2013 Benz.

"Yeah! Today can't get any better!"

I got another gift out of the mail box; from Memorial Dr., in Decatur, GA. I opened my letter. I was as happy as a six foot tall bull frog! I read it:

Nobody's Perfect

But you are perfect for me.
I can't wait to show you, when I get free.
I know we have our ups and downs.
I know we have our smiles and frowns.
Sometimes we feel like giving up.
But God made us strong and tuff.
One day, I will hold your hand.
Make love to you, and be your man.
Kiss you from your head, to the bottom of your feet.
Rub you, and feel your body heat.
No more arguing, pressure and stress.
Just us against the world, baby you are the best.
One day we will be on T.V., with riches and fame
Taking pictures with our book, and signing autographs
     of our name
You leaving me while I'm down, would be like Tiny
     leaving T.I.

<u>I'm your king, and you're my Ride or Die!</u>
<u>I love you, stay down, and your reward will come in</u>
<u>millions when I'm free.</u>
<u>God knows, the first time we looked in each other's</u>
<u>eyes, I knew I was perfect for you, and you were</u>
<u>perfect for me!!!</u>

Aww. My man really had such a way with words. Tears of lonely love, came down my pretty face. I missed him. I loved him. His words, poems, and voice. He could be so charming. I loved this man!

"God, please bring my man home!" I laid on the bed, and listened to Keri Hilson.

"Hey!"

"What the? Hey!"

It was Joe! He was in my face. Then in my arms, then lying on top of me, kissing me. He had been gone three months. I never missed a visit; wrote a letter every week. Accepted every phone call.

Now it was all over, and it was on and popping! I was getting a refill of his love. Fresh out of jail sex was the best! He held me, like a man, mixed with the power of a bear. He stroked like a lion, but had that burning passion at the same dang time. I was on my back. He was on top of me; pulling my hair, staring into my eyes, and making me melt like butter!

Trey Songz played on repeat,

"Girl you gone think, you gone think I invented sex!"

Yes Lord! I think he did invent it! Wooh! Good tootey of fruity! He smacked my booty!

We broke the sex record, and created new positions! We did it Froggy style and Doggy style at the same dang time! After twenty-four straight hours of love, I wanted to lock him back up! This was too good, cause he slept with me for two straight days! I just rested on his tight, tatted up chest.

"Baby, get up."

"Excuse you?"

"Damn, Erica. Give a nigga some space. I been laid up with you for two damn days. I been missing money!"

I watched this dog get up, shower and leave like last year! Didn't hear from that fool no more that night! I called; he ignored. Finally, he picked up.

"Erica! Stop calling! Police is hot out here!"

"Joe, baby . . ." I started, but he hung up.

DON'T MAKE LOVE IN THE CLUB

Joe was in the hypest club in Augusta. He was in the corner with a cute yellow girl, with his hands up her short skirt. She was grinding and bending over on him. He was hunching her and getting her high, freaky, and drunk at the same dang time. The girl was so easy. She was super drunk. He slid her a pill, and then slid inside her.

"Biiiiietch!"

"Stop! Baby, no!"

"No, nothing nigga!"

"Who, who, who is she?" The drunk, high freak asked.

"This the slut that's about to beat yo freaky, nasty ass!" I yelled, and kicked the stuttering, drunk slut in the stomach.

"Ouch . . ." she whimpered.

"Not feeling so slutty now huh?!"

Slap!

I slapped her so hard, a tooth came out.

"Since you naked, show the world, girl!" I said, snatching her skirt down. She didn't have on any panties!

"Dang! My Bad!"

She smelled like a dead cat, with fish stuck in her butt! She smelled so bad, the entire club got foggy. Like her funky couchie sprayed some funky couchie pepper spray! The whole club was coughing!

"What the hell is that smell?" D.J. asked.

"Is it a dead body in here?" JB asked.

"Who havin' sex wit' a crack head?" Chi asked.

"Are yall blowing fart out the speakers?" Scott joked.

"Good Lawd! I smell fish foot!" C'yera said, sneezing from the skunk couchie.

"Damn, if yall want to close down the club, find a better way to do it than throwing invisible shit balls!" Reece said, holding his nose.

If they only knew, that was the putty cat they smelled. People were holding their noses, and pushing themselves out the club!

Bam!

"What the?" I asked feeling a fist punch me in the back of my head.

"That's my sister, trick!" Some dude named Ced had hit me! I guess the yellow, stanking, no pantie wearing tramp was his sister.

Bam! Bam!

Joe punched Ced two times and knocked out two teeth!

"Ouch! Trick! My balls!" Ced cried.

Yeah, I kicked the minute man smack dead in the balls!

Bang! Push! Smack!

A girl punched me, and another girl grabbed my throat. Three dudes with dreads were fighting Joe.

Now we were both getting jumped on, in this country club, in Augusta with no one to help! Why did I follow Joe to the club?!

Bang! Crack!

Glass broke over her head.

"Yeah, hoe! Leave my girl alone!"

Kenya PimpCity Always Fighting Brown was there again. She cracked a large bottle of Patron over the two-hundred-eight-five pound gorilla look alike, girl's head that was choking me.

Now I was ready to practice the karate I learned when I was in the fifth grade at Coan Middle School! I got my Matrix on. I jumped on top of the table and back kicked the girl in her right eye! Yeah, I learned that move from Will Smith's son. Then me and Kenya helped Joe.

Pow! Slash! Boom!

"Damn, Kenya! You can't shoot at people in the club!"

"Damn Joe! You can't screw people in the club!" I said after I cut dude's ear off with my box cutter. He let my man go quick, when his left ear fell on the damn dance floor!

We ran out of the club, then jumped in our rides and left. We met up at the Ramada Inn Hotel, on Gordon Highway.

Joe and I made love, while Kenya chilled with Mr. Pimp City in the next room, counting thousands, and smoking on two pounds of Keysha.

"What's my name?! What's my name?! Joe yelled as he beat my beat up!

IN JESUS NAME

Early that Sunday morning, we decided to go to church. Of course, Joe didn't stay long. He left, time I sat down!

Reverend Bobby Brown was the pastor of Saint John's Baptist Church. I loved my pastor, jerry curls and all! He made you feel the Word in your bones!

"By the blood of Jesus, you are healed! In Jesus blood, we are saved! By Jesus blood, we are alive! In the name of Jesus, we are blessed! We are blessed when we come, and we are blessed when we go!"

He preached that word, in his purple and gold suit. He walked back and forth. He had wet curls, and wore expensive Gucci glasses. His purple Stacy Adams shoes were gleaming. The six foot-two inch, two-hundred and fifty pound Rev. Bobby Brown continued to preach as he wiped the sweat off of his face, with his purple rag.

"The disciples couldn't understand why their prayers were not strong enough to heal the little boy. They asked Jesus why their prayers didn't run the evil spirit out. Jesus replied in Mark 9:29: "This kind of power comes only by prayer and fasting.""

I sat there, and I prayed for my sister-in-law, Daja. She had gotten shot fighting with me, over a nigga that I just caught humping in the club, with a stranger! This was not worth her life.

"Lord, don't let Daja die", I closed my eyes and prayed.

"Jesus said, I tell you the truth. If two of you on Earth pray together and agree on anything! Not some things, but anything! All God needs is two of you to agree! Jesus said, it will be done for you! He will make it happen! Matthew 18:19-20. When two or three come together in Jesus name! I said, come together in Jesus name! He will do it!"

"Amen."

"Huh?" I jumped, shocked to see Joe sitting behind me.

We left the church, and drove to Grady Hospital, to visit his sister.

"Hey girl, what it do?" Kenya asked. She was reading her pink women's bible to Daja. Her man, Mr. Pimp City was sitting down watching ESPN.

"How is she doing?" I asked.

"Not good at all. I'm her RN. I'm afraid she hasn't responded to anything. I think she is a vegetable."

"What the hell you call my sister? A vegetable? Are you tryna joke at a time like this, by calling my sister a banana or some collard greens?!" Joe asked like an idiot.

I giggled. Kenya looked at him and smiled. Pimp shook his head and kept watching the NFL news.

"No, a vegetable means brain dead," the nurse replied.

"Noooooo!" Joe went crazy!

"Sir, calm down."

Bam!

Joe picked the T.V. up, and threw it out the window! Two officers ran in.

"Sir! Sir! What's the problem?"

"Oh, it's ok," the RN lied.

"Let's all pray," I suggested, in the heat of the moment.

"Good idea," the white cop said.

"True," Pimp said, getting up probably praying that he could finish watching Sports Center on the T.V. in his car, since Joe threw the hospital T.V. out the window!

We all prayed, and held hands. Me, Joe, Kenya PimpCity Brown, Mr. Pimp City, RN Bailey, and the two cops.

"Lord, we all come to you, and we need a miracle. You said if two or more come to you, and ask anything, anything, You would do it. Lord, we are asking in Jesus name, for you to heal Daja."

There was silence.

"Erica? Why are you crying? You have any gummy bears?"

"Huh? Oh, Lord!" I was so shocked and happy! Daja woke up! We all laughed, and hugged each other.

"What's the hype about? Did someone get married?" Daja asked, still not realizing where she was.

"It's a miracle! We thought we would have to pull the plug." RN Bailey said.

"No the hell you wasn't pulling no plug on my sister. I woulda shot every doctor in this muther!"

"Oh my God? What happened to me?" Daja started panicking and snatching off the cords.

"Stop, honey! Calm down," the nurse said.

We all tried to calm her down.

"It's ok, its ok, boo boo," I said, hugging my beautiful sister-in-law.

I sat on her bed, and we both cried as I rocked her in my arms.

SAME OLD STUFF, DIFFERENT DAY

M e, Daja, Kenya, and my twin sister Keysha was chilling at my house eating three large pizzas. I was at my piano, playing Alicia Keys. Me and my singing niece, Bre'Shauna, were singing perfect together,

> "Some people want it all,
> But I don't want nothing at all,
> If it ain't you, baby
> If I ain't got you baby."

"Some people want yall to shut the hell up! Damn! I'm cooking dope!" Joe yelled like an angry stepfather!

"Baby, why you cussing around Bre'Shauna?"

"This my damn house. All yall can get the hell out!"

"Hold up, Joe." I stood up.

He looked like he was about to swing.

"Joe, Erica, chill out," my uncle Chicago said, walking in through the patio, leaving his black Lexus running.

Bre'Shauna ran and gave uncle Chi a big hug.

"Hey, let's just leave." I decided. We all left Joe's crazy butt in the kitchen with his cooking ass! We went to the Wal-Mart in Lithonia.

"What's up, Sexy Chocolate?" a tall, brown sugar smooth dude asked me.

"Hmmm. Nothin." I said, noticing he looked like Will Smith.

"Hold up, ain't you Joe's girl?" he asked.

"Well of course. Why?"

"Oh, so you know what just happened, about five minutes ago?" he asked.

"What?"

"He got killed," the dude said, and walked off.

"Oh, God! Joe!"

I ran like that Jamaican dude in the 2012 Summer Olympics!

Me, Kenya, and the girls, all jumped in my new Cadillac truck.

No one talked. It was so quiet, you could hear an ant fart.

Poof!—Is how it woulda sounded.

No music or nothing. I was shaking and crying. I loved this man, with his arrogant ego, and his mean swagged ass! He was my Chris Brown with a Fifty-cent body, and Stacy Dash eyes!

We got there . . . . Boom! I hit the curve. Fuck it! I jumped out. We all ran in. The door was open. The lights were off. I was scared of what I would see. I cut the living room light on, then the kitchen light.

"Blood!" Kenya said.

Then I saw it. Blood was on our snow white couch! I held my chest, and went to my room. I knew it! All the wrong my man did, had finally caught up with him. Someone had paid him back.

Tick. Tick.

I pushed the door open.

"Punk! Biiiitch!" I yelled.

He was knocked out sleep and drunk, at the same dang time! He had some big booty slut lying on his chest! It was on! This time, I hit his drunk ass.

Bam!

I punched his ass, and cat woman kicked his trick!

He tried to react, but the liquor had him moving slower than Uncle Sam's grandma! I just got on top of him, and beat his ass! I cried with every swing! He embarrassed me in front of my friends!

Bam! "You Dog!"

Bang! "You Punk!"

Wack! "You Trick!"

Bam! "You Junglenut!"

"Get him, girl!" Daja cheered.

I looked back at his sister, and winked my eye, then punched him like it was the Fourth of July!

Kah Boom!

Joe was bleeding like a boxer and a bulldog, in a ten minute street fight! His slut was trying to put on her clothes and leave.

Smack!

Keysha back slapped her.

"Naw, hold on sis. I want her head up. So, Miss New Booty. You want to hump my man, on my bed, in my house?!"

Pow!

"What the?"

Kenya PimpCity Brown, just shot the chick in the head like we was in a damn video game!

"Kenya? Are you nuts?!" I asked my best friend.

"Naw, that slut was nuts," Kenya said, laughing.

"Let's drag this hoe in the closet," Kenya said.

"Great idea," Daja agreed, pushing the closet open.

"Noooo!" A female yelled.

"Who the hell are you?" Daja asked.

"Oh know he didn't! Slut, why you in my shit naked?! He had a threesome!?" I yelled.

"I, I, I didn't mean it."

POW. POW. POW.

"I didn't mean to shoot you three times in your couchie, trick!" I yelled.

Damn, Kenya PimpCity Brown was wearing off on me!

"What the hell we gonna do with these hoes?" Keysha asked.

"Throw them in the ocean," my niece said.

"What the hell? Where did you come from, Bre'Shauna?"

"I forgot my purse, aunty. Sorry," she said, and walked away.

"Yall ladies leave."

Boom!

"I will take care of these hoes," my Uncle Chicago said.

Uncle Chi, blew the girl I that I had just shot, head clean off her body! He was a real Gangster Disciple from Chitown. He knew how to erase a body from the earth.

It was quiet. Gospel music time! I turned it on, and I prayed. This man was driving me crazy! Making me turn into a damn cow girl.

Yeeeee Haahhh!!!

NIGGAS AND FLIES!

"Why do men cheat?" I asked my girls.

"Hell, I ain't a man," Keysha said, and we all laughed.

"You know, a good man is hard to find. Sometimes I think a good man is impossible to find. I want me an Obama!" Kenya shouted. We gave her a high five!

"Girl, niggas ain't shit," Daja said. She looked beautiful. You couldn't even tell she had been shot.

"I just don't understand men. I give him my all, he gives me his balls!" I said, causing us to burst out laughing.

"Ha, ha. Girl, you crazy. Men are full of shit! That's why I stayed single for a year. But Erica, you always got me. I got your back." Kenya told me.

"Yea, Hun. You got my back. I'm so happy to have the Female Scare Face, Nino Brown, Kenya PimpCity Brown on my side!" I said, and we all laughed.

"Hell naw, you too funny. Girl, I just don't take no shit. I been through a lot, with men my whole life," Kenya said.

"I been raped by my own father!" Keysha said.

Bam!

I slapped her tongue ring out! Her mouth was bleeding like a slit wrist!

"Bietch! Don't you ever talk about my daddy! He ain't never touched your blow torch pussy! You know what?! I shoulda whipped your ass when you fucked my man!"

Bang! Bang! Zap!

Yeah, I beat her ass Batman style! I didn't feel sorry for her! Hell, I was still mad she could beat me, when we were young. I was still mad her butt was an inch bigger than mine!

I elbowed her in the chin. Bam!

I kicked her in the head, then grabbed her hair, and slung her through the air, over the dining room table. BAM!

Her back hit the wall like a pancake. I was her frying pan!

Ding!

I smacked her on the top of the head with the frying pan! I was hurt. All the years Keysha beat me up. All the times she got the most attention. Then she screwed my baby daddy/man! This bo-legged, freaky, jelly booty, stripper body-having slut, had the nerves to talk bad about our daddy! In front of these girls!

Bang!

I kicked her in her tiny stomach. Time to stomp her to death! Who cares?! I was on a kill a punk, slut roll today!

I held my leg high up in the air, like the female Incredible Hulk.

"Stop!" Daja said, grabbing my leg, causing me to fall to the ground.

"Let her be!" Kenya yelled at Daja, pushing her.

"What?!" No you didn't just push me!"

"Yes, I did! So what you gone do, cause I will slap your yellow ass from Atlanta to Seattle!"

"Try it! You touch me again; I will break your face, nose, and tongue! Country, crazy, two dollar hoe!" Daja snapped back at Kenya.

The two yellow bones were face to face, like two heavy weight boxers. Neither would back down. Their noses were touching. They were both sweating and breathing hard, like track stars!

Woosh!

Daja drew the first blood. She pushed Kenya down to the ground, and went for the A-town stomp!

"Ooops!" Daja shouted.

Kenya caught her leg, and snatched her up in the air. Wham! Daja hit the floor!

Kenya jumped on top of her like an ant on chocolate.

Bam! Bam!

Daja ate those two punches and Bam! She flipped Kenya PimpCity Brown, and got on top of her like a lion.

Bam! Bam!

Daja hit her hard two times.

Bam!

Kenya flipped her, but Daja held her hands.

POW!

"Damn." Is all I could say. Kenya PimpCity Brown, my best friend, just shot my sister. She nearly killed my sister!

"Break it up!"

All heads turned backwards. It was my favorite Uncle Chicago again!

Kenya and Daja looked up at him.

"Get off me!" Daja yelled, pushing Kenya off of her.

Uncle Chi is the one who shot the gun.

"Yall just chill. Why are yall fighting?!" Uncle Chi asked.

"And who the hell rearranged Keysha face?!" he asked.

"Boop!" Me, Kenya, and Daja said at the same dang time!

MAKE UP TO BREAK UP

A week ago, we were all on each other like flies on crap! Today, we were all laughing and playing Spades.

"Renig! Caught you, Daja!" I yelled.

"Ha, ha. Naw, bet two books." Daja challenged me.

"I know you just cut diamonds, now you are playing diamonds. You owe us three books." I demanded.

"Yeah, give us our books," my spade partner, Kenya said.

"Bang!" Daja flipped over all of her books. All eyes were on those eight cards.

"Dang! Ha, ha! Buttermilk, butt bread!" I joked. We all laughed.

"Told yall hoes. I cut hearts! Give me MY books!" Daja joked.

She and Keysha beat us two games in a row after we put the Michael Jackson 5 straight glove on them!

"I love you," a male voice said, placing his arms around my neck. He had on some nice cologne.

Dam ham of Sam. I melted.

It was my man. Looking good as a million bucks!

"Excuse us." I said, as he picked me up in his strong arms, and carried me to the bedroom like a princess.

He laid me down on my back. I ripped his Polo, button up shirt off, felt on his chest, and wrapped my slim fit legs around him. I bit my lip, curled my toes, and closed my eyes.

He began to take me on a hard, fast, deep, good, and painful ride!

One thing he could do, is put it down! But, when I woke up, I felt funny, and weird. He was knocked out, snoring like a polar bear in Alaska with purple socks and a pink thong on!

"Dammit man!"

I threw up all over the bathroom. I felt dizzy, like I was about to faint. I was down on my knees, throwing up in the toilet.

I couldn't utter a word. I just laid there on my back, holding my super small model stomach. It didn't look like I had gained any weight with my pregnancy. I dealt with the intense pain until I went to sleep.

"Get your butt up." Joe said.

"Oh, baby . . . take me to the hospital," I whined.

"Tell your girlfriend to take you." Joe said, and left me on the damn floor!

That damn dog!

I crawled in the bedroom and got on the phone. I dialed the number.

"What's up, babes?"

"Girl, my stomach hurt. Drive me to Grady."

"Ok boo, be there is a sec," Kenya said.

She came in, and helped me walk to the truck.

"You ok baby?" A cool white boy named Scott asked. He lived across the street. He was always cool as ice to me.

"I'm good buddy."

"OK lil mama. I'm here if you need me," he said. Then he went back in his yard with D.J. and Champ.

I was stretched out on the back seat, while Kenya drove to the hospital.

"So, what do you think is wrong?" she asked.

"Girl, I'm in too much pain. I don't know."

"Well, Ima be here for you girl, as a friend, but you can't let him stress you out. Beyoncé said we run the world, girl!"

"Ha, ha. That's funny, Kenya. Truth be told, this nigga is super stressing me out."

"Girl, I see why some women turn gay! Niggas just act like dogs! Roof! Roof!" Kenya said laughing.

"Girl, so true."

"Erica, I love you girl. My chocolate Nicki Minaj."

"Heee, hee, girl you too funny, Mariah Carey," I joked back.

Kenya was cheering me up. Laughter is good medicine.

Too much nigga stress. I can't make this nigga do right for nothing! But why am I doing so right? 'Cause I love him.

"You love him a lot, don't you?"

"You know it."

"Always love yourself first. Every man I ever met tried to fuck me," Kenya said, as she puffed on the blunt.

"Yeah, nothing new. All dogs go to hell!" I laughed.

But I felt the same way. I wish he was better; giving a slut at least fifty percent!

"We here, boo," Kenya said.

She tried to help me out.

"I'm good. You can leave. Ima call him to pick me up."

"You sure?"

"Positive."

"OK, Hun. Call me," Kenya PimpCity Brown said, backing up.

"Freeze! I'll blow your head off!" a young, white dude said, with a gun to Kenya's head. He had to be about nineteen, and high as a kite. He was young, and skinny, and he had on a T-shirt and dirty blue jeans.

He snatched the door open when she was looking at me. He looked deranged. Murder was boiling in his eyes. I had to think quick.

"So, Mr. Serial Killer, what you gonna do? Shoot me, or kiss me?" Kenya Pimp City Brown said, staring the young serial killer dead in his eyes.

"Neither. Ima rape you, and cut your throat, after I shoot you in the head!"

POW!

No! No! No! This was not supposed to happen! Not like this. I felt so bad. Terrible! How could God allow this?

I couldn't accept it. I had killed a man.

BOOP!

"Get your dead ass out of my Cadillac truck!" Kenya PimpCity Brown said, pushing his limp body on the pavement.

"You good?" I asked.

"Yea girl, I wasn't scared. Great job. You learning."

"Ha, ha, I don't like killing. That was my first."

"Ha, ha, well, tah, tah, tah. You Booped him!" she said, driving off fast, blasting Luda's old song, 'Move Slut (Get out the Way).'

I had to laugh, he was my first kill. But at the rate Joe was going, he wouldn't be my last!

Cling. Cling.

I threw the silver .380 in the trash, after I wiped it down. Lord, forgive me, but that was self-defense, I told myself. I still didn't feel any better though.

"I'm very sorry, Miss Brown. Take these pills, and the STD will go away," the pretty white nurse Micky said.

"Naw, I'm killing this nigga to sleep!" I said, angry as a pit bull with peanut butter in his nose!

"Your baby is healthy, and won't be affected. Your fine. Just have protected sex with your partner," she said.

Blah. Blah. Blah.

That was the last straw. I'm about to Freddy Krueger this nigga! I snatched the medicine out of her hand, ignored her little stupid health tip, and called my homeboy, J.B. to pick me up. Of course, he got there in two minutes! He been dying to taste this cherry!

"What's up, lil buddy?" J.B., who's black and Chinese asked.

He had gotten out of prison yesterday. He paroled out of Albany State, ran his stack up to $50,000, and bought a new Dodge Charger, all black.

"Just take me home."

"Bet." Those were the only words we exchanged.

He played T.I., and jumped onto I-20.

We were almost there.

"There he go! Follow him!" I yelled.

He looked at me funny, then tailed behind him. Joe was in the Maybach, windows tinted.

We stayed at least two car lengths behind him. We followed him down Glenwood, to Covington Highway, and followed him to some apartments, near Prime Time.

I felt something bad was about to happen. I knew it! Instincts are never wrong. Then again . . . .

"You cool?" J.B. asked.

"Yea, let me out. I'll call you if I need you," I told him. I could feel his eyes watching my butt, as I walked off. Joe had pulled up and parked.

I watched him go inside apartment C-4. J.B. dropped me off, one building down, and I walked up to the apartment. I heard crying.

I pushed the door; it was half-way open.

"Joe!"

He was shocked. For the first time, I could look in his eyes, and tell he was embarrassed.

"Who baby you holding?" I asked.

"Mine," a female replied.

"And who are you? Joe, what . . ."

I was too hurt to be shocked. I was too hurt to fight. All the fight had drained out of my body.

"The ba, baby? How old is he?" I asked, shuttering and shaking. My legs were getting weak.

"Two months, and my name is Mungie," the big booty girl said.

"Really, Joe?" I asked, waiting on him to put up some kind of defense or response. Nothing. Not a word.

"Nigga! I'm two months pregnant with your second baby, and all you can do is stand here like a fool! And on top of that, we lost our first son because you stomped me in the stomach! And you over here holding this chick baby?!"

I was heated. Now I was in killer mode; all the way turned up. Somebody had to pay! Him, her, and the damn baby!

I looked around the living room. There were expensive baby clothes everywhere!

"Well, I guess he didn't tell you he was leaving you either. But he is. Man up, Joe." Mungie said. She gave me an evil grin, then continued to burst my bubble.

"And tell her how every night you come over here. Tell her how you say my sex is more exciting. Tell her how you say you killed her baby on purpose. Tell her how much money you give me. Erica, he been paying my rent for two years! And he . . ."

Smack!

That was enough. The gorilla booty trick was popping off at the mouth a little too much! I snatched all her weave out. I looked at her red weave, spit on it, and threw it in the kitchen sink.

Ping!

Yep, I hit the bald head, big mouth tramp across the head with the frying pan. Then I kicked her in the stomach, and shoved her on the floor. She was crying, and her punk ass baby was crying at the same dang time. She and the baby were both bald headed; like a baby's booty.

I got on top of Mungie. "Now slut, you wanna sit here and brag. Think you gonna destroy my relationship, and take my man? I want you to run and tell this!" I roared, like a female lion.

Slice. Slice. Slice.

"Ahhh! Joe! Get this crazy slut off me!" she screamed.

"I bet you won't screw nobody else man! This mine! My property! After I get done cutting your pretty face, you gonna look like Chucky vs. Freddy at the same dang time!"

"Help! Noooo! Joe!" she cried.

Joe just held the baby, while I sliced the slut nose off!!! I cut Mungie so many times, her face looked like a baseball glove inside of old, tore-up stockings!

"You're out, hoe!" I shouted, and slapped Joe's ass! Then I snatched his keys, jumped in his Maybach, and drove downtown to the first bar I saw, on Peach Street-Hooters! Perfect!

HOOTERS

I sat inside Hooters, ate hot wings, and got sloppy drunk. I didn't give a damn if I crashed that nigga's car! Fuck him and his car at the same dang time!

"Nigga, you ain't Rick Ross! You ain't the boss!" I yelled at nobody, as I laid my head down in my arms and cried myself to sleep.

"Excuse me, Miss. We're closed. Are you, ok? I've been trying to wake you up for some time now," my waitress said.

"A, ah, hmm. Who cooked pig feet tonight? Did my mom slap that monkey? I told that damn dog Cup Cake! Cup Cake! Come here you little Biiietch!" I said sloppy drunk.

I was tore up from the floor up, talking out of my head.

"Miss, Ima hafta help you. You are tore up, baby. You look like Kill Bill after her fight with Vivica Fox and the ball chain, girl!" the waitress continued.

"Are you driving?" she asked.

I nodded my head, yea.

"Well, I can drive you home 'cause my cousin, Pop, dropped me off."

I still didn't answer, I just tossed her the keys. She walked behind the restaurant. "Where's your car? Did someone steal it? There is no car out here," the waitress said.

I was too drunk to respond. I stumbled, and she caught me. I looked up, and spotted my slick, candy apple, candy coated Maybach. I pointed towards it.

"Ha, ha. You are pretty damn drunk! Girl, that's probably the President's car, or Will Smith's ride."

I nodded my head, in a weak gesture, raised my arms, aimed at the car, and opened the car doors. They swung open, and the Rick Ross song came on.

'Maybach music . . .'

The waitress was stunned! She started stuttering like she was drunk now!

"Well, I be damned, girl. Are you T.I. daughter?" she asked.

"Ha, ha, I wish, girl. I'm Chris Brown daughter. The street Chris Brown, not the singer/actor."

"Oh wow. Breezy did it hard! Dang girl, you got real fur seats! And a leopard floor! And a cool tint, platinum rims . . . Wooh! Hook me up. He got any friends?" she asked.

"Ha, ha. Yea. Ima hook you up with his best friend, Trapp." I told her.

"Oh, girl, that's what's up. My name Porsche. I'm from Detroit. The big-D, baby!" she shouted and laughed.

I never looked at her, actually. I decided to check her out. She had naturally long hair, honey brown skin, no belly, and a dynamic, curvy bottom. I could hang with her. She was fine, like me. I hadn't been doing my squats, but my thighs were track star tight. My stomach was super model perfect, my butt was Nicki Minaj thick, and of course, my face was movie star pretty.

"Like, where do you live?" Porsche asked.

"Oh, just take me to a hotel."

"Ok, is this one straight?" she asked, pulling into the Marriot.

"Biiitch! Watch where you going!" a black, burnt French toast-faced dude with glasses said. He was driving a new truck.

He had almost hit us, when Porsche made a sharp turn into the hotel.

"Hold on, hun." Porsche said, and got out the car.

She slowly walked to his window. It was already rolled down.

"Listen, nigga. I got yo Biiitch!" Porsche said with a butcher knife as long as a miniature bat to his face.

He pissed on himself, and melted like butter. He went from Incredible Hulk to Mighty Mouse in two seconds!

"Now, you got that!" Miss Detroit said, poking his face with her middle finger, and I'm not talking about a Facebook poke!

I'm talking about, she poked blood out of the nigga face with her long nails! She walked back to the pimp ride, and got in.

"Sorry, hun. You know us Detroit girls don't play."

I nodded, and passed out.

The only thing I remembered, is waking up.

"Awww, the princess finally woke up," Porsche said smiling, with perfect white teeth.

She had a one-thousand dollar bottle of red wine, and some chocolate cake, cake, cake, cake, cake! She was blasting that old Chris Brown and Rihanna 'Birthday Cake' song.

"What time is it?" I asked Porsche.

"It's five pm, two days later! I done been to work, twice, and you still ain't moved! You been knocked out like dinosaur couchie!" Porsche said, laughing.

"What?" I was stunned; like a football player being caught cheating and getting sweet potatoes stuck up his butt!

I just scratched my wild, soft hair. I looked around the room, still half sleep; my eyes trying to adjust to the light. I was trying to remember why in the jail house, ramen noodle soup hell, I was in a hotel room with another chick!

"Hold up! Are yall robbing me?" I asked Porsche.

"Ha, ha. Why would you think that?" Porsche asked.

"Well, who is that with that big ass gun?" I asked confused, and worried while rubbing my eyes.

"Oh, that's my home girl, Awesome Ashley, from Griffin," Porsche said.

"So what. I'm Erica Hustle-N-Flow Brown, and this don't feel right. Why is she sitting there with a long shot gun? I may look like Nikki Minaj, but I'm not! Why in the hell do I got a body guard?" I asked sitting up in the bed with my red Victoria Secret bra, showing my nice sized breasts.

"Look, I couldn't leave you here alone; a beautiful drunk female? You was knocked out like gorilla breath! I had to go to work, so I told Ashley to watch you."

"Really? How sweet. But what if Awesome Ashley would have killed me or shot me," I complained.

"Like this?!!"

Boom! Boom! Boom!

Gunshots.

"Did I get shot this time?"

Bam!

Suddenly, the lights went off.

The door swung open. The lights flashed on. There were three men, dressed in black, with masks on. Next thing I knew, Ashley was tied up, and Porsche was on the floor, dead, I guess. She wasn't moving.

"You! Where the money at? Or this one hundred and twenty pound, brown sugar friend of yours is dead," the four hundred pound masked man said, holding a gun in Ashley's mouth.

"Ouch!" he hollered.

Ashley kicked him in the balls. Wow. She was bold. How in the cabbage town hell did she find his balls? He was four hundred pounds with three bellies!

Boom! Boom!

The other guy hit the ground. Then the four hundred pounder fell to the ground. Blood was coming out of his mouth like a water fountain, from the shot in his back that blew out his chest!

"Yea biiiitch!!! I'm here again! I got a room next door, and heard the noise!" Kenya PimpCity Brown said.

She was standing there in all black, wearing a wife beater, skin tight pants, and black boots. I just looked at her, and shook my head. She had on a red bandana, 'cause her husband was a blood. She was standing there with her man's double barrel shot gun in her hand like the female Nino Brown. I was beginning to believe she was my Ghetto Angel, and my best friend all in one.

Porsche got up. She was playing dead.

"Nice to meet you, I'm Ashley, from Griffin, GA," the cutie said, shaking my hand.

I smiled, almost laughed, feeling ashamed that I had slept so damn long, with this pretty little angel watching my beautiful, helpless body.

"Cool, I'm Erica Hustle-N-Flow Brown, from downtown." I said, and we all laughed.

"And who are you, Cat Woman?" Porsche asked Kenya.

"Naw, baby. You joking right?" Kenya asked, as she laughed out loud.

"You ain't heard of me? I'm the wife of a living legend. The creator of the Pimp City East Side Drug Family. Like Nino Brown. I'm Kenya PimpCity Brown."

"And I'm the police. Freeze!"

There were ten Atlanta police officers in the room.

"Cuff her."

"What?! I'm innocent! Hell naw! I ain't do shit!" I yelled in anger.

No way! I wasn't going for this. Jackie Chan taught me this.

Wham!

I jumped up, and kicked the seven foot tall officer right in the nose! Bam! The giant fell down.

Bam. Bam. Bang. Kick. Punch.

Three cops rushed me. I did a round house and back kicked all three, dropping them like flies. Bam! I kicked the lady officer. I was the top karate kid in Georgia, and I still had it, baby!

"Four down, six to go!" Kenya said.

Bang! Kenya smacked the short officer in the nose.

"Ouch! Good God! My God!" the other white officer yelled, after Ashley kicked him in his ding dong.

Whap!

Porsche knocked the other officer out with a lamp.

"Damn it." I said.

I ran, jumped up, and kicked two cops, at the same dang time, each with one leg! I did a split in the air!

Wow. I thought I had forgotten that move.

"Now you!" I yelled at a slim, black officer.

All four of us surrounded him.

"Look, Shawty, I'm from Decatur. I ain't no hater. I will just say the two dead dudes went crazy and I saved the day," the brown-skinned officer said. He looked like Juvenile, with Lil Wayne's hair!

"Great, cause I got you recorded on my phone. So if we go down, you go down, compliments of Erica Hustle-N-Flow Brown." I said, and we all walked out, like we were leaving the club.

"Damn!" Ashley screamed.

"What now?" I asked.

"Who we gotta kill?" Kenya asked.

"Nobody. I broke a nail." Ashley said.

We all laughed. I jumped in my candy apple, rich nigga swag, Maybach. Yea, Rick Ross style.

Kenya jumped into a yellow, new Maserati. Where the hell did she get that from? Oh well, maybe that's another story.

The new chick, Ashley jumped into a purple Lamborghini.

Then Porsche . . . no she didn't boo, boo! Yes she did! This chick jumped into a money green helicopter with tinted windows, and dollar signs all over it!

I'm just thinking, we beat up the Cops and the Robbers and the same damn time! Yeah! The REAL Bad Girl's Club!

HERE WE GO AGAIN

I was glad the ten officers were too embarrassed to admit that four, fine, black girls whipped their tussys!

I was feeling myself, listening to T.I. 'What You Know About That,' pulling up in my neighborhood like I knew I was the shit!

"What the hell?"

I almost swallowed my tongue ring!

"This slut made nigga! He just keep trying me!"

I had to close my eyes, rub them, blink them fast, and open them up again. I couldn't believe this ice-cream booty nigga! He had my red Benz that he bought on my birthday, parked in another slut's driveway, two houses down from me.

I politely parked, and got out.

Tap. Tap. Tap.

Waited. Nothing. One minute. Two minutes,

"Mother fu !"

"Who is it?" a female asked me.

"It's your mama," I said being smart.

"Mom!" the girl said, and swung the door open.

I swung and stopped my fist at her jaw.

"Ashley? From the hotel?"

"Erica Hustle-N-Flow Brown?"

"What the hell are you doing here?"

"My sister, Crystal, lives here."

"Well, where is my nigga?" I asked quickly getting back into beast mode.

"He back there," Ashley said, feeling like, 'Ahh, shit! Its bout to go down!'

I walked down the hall with my box cutter in my hand, pregnant, and beginning to show. I was stressing like a wild street hoe, and so tired of all this fighting. I ain't the black Wonder Woman! Or was I?

I didn't want to lose this baby over no nigga, but a slut gets tired.

"Nasty Nigga!"

He was on his knees, eating gummy bears out of her couchie!

Kick. Stomp. Smack.

I kicked him in the back of the head, causing him to choke on a red gummy bear, and a pink pussy cat, at the same dang time.

"Hey, I'm innocent. I had no idea this cat licker was your man." Crystal said, with nothing but a pink Victoria Secret bra on, and legs still open.

I just looked at her, shook my head, and walked out.

"Always blame the nigga," Ashley said.

"I know, right? But Ash, I'm starting to blame myself for letting this nigga dog me like this," I said.

I heard loud, crushing, powerful thunder and lightning. Rain started dropping down hard like bricks. The sky became Alaska dark as I ran and hopped into my Maybach.

"Dam! That quick . . ." I ran my fingers through my hair. Yep, my hair was totaled like a car accident!

"Now what?"

Thank God for Russell Simmons and Kimora! I grabbed my Pink Baby Phat rain Jacket, held it over my head, and ran into my house.

"Enuff!" I cried.

I was breaking down. I was stumbling through the house in tears. Grabbing all of his shit, and throwing it out the house. I grabbed his two-thousand dollar Armani shirts, his tan pair of brand new Polo boots, his new Akoo outfits, and his nine-hundred dollar cologne. Everything had to go! Whack!

"Straight up! Mob shit!" I yelled. Like my cousin San would say. I was in my moment thinking about the ATL, Mob family.

Like Keri Hilson said, every woman has a breaking point. But R. Kelly said it best. When a woman's fed up . . .

Dog, I'm pregnant! I started feeling dizzy. I was still crying. My stomach was hurting like a slut! I held my belly, and got down on my knees at the foot of my queen sized bed. I cuddled with my Mickey Mouse blanket. I didn't feel happy like the kids in Disney World now. I felt hopeless. This was my first love. Not only that, he was the only man that I had ever slept with. I was hurting mentally, physically, emotionally, now spiritually.

"God . . ."

I cried and prayed. This had to end. "Lord, it gotta get greater later . . ."

"Get her! Get her! Rush her to the hospital! We're losing her! We're losing her!" the pretty, petite paramedic yelled.

I could see the commotion. However, I was quickly fading away. I was just lucky enough to dial 911. This nigga was killing me, literally!

I woke up in the hospital room, for the hundredth time!

"Baby, I'm sorry. I love you."

I looked up, and it was him, the devil himself. The devil in red. The dragon faced, cheating, no good, handsome bastard!

"I love you." Joe said again, high as a kite, on a windy day, in Chicago! I couldn't speak.

"When does she leave?" he asked the nurse, Alishia.

"A few days sir." the stunning, Asian nurse replied.

"Well baby, I love you, and I just wanted to show you some love. I will come back tomorrow." he said.

'Ridin 'round wit' that Nina! Ridin wit' a hoe named Keysha, smokin' on Keysha!' The blasting ring tone of his phone went off.

"I gotta go. Trap music, boo," Joe said, running out of the room, without even kissing me.

"Excuse you!" Ashley said, as Joe knocked her back while he was running out of the room and she was coming in.

"My bad. What's up lil mama?" Joe asked.

"Nigga please," Crystal said, rolling her eyes.

Now this slut had some balls and some nuts at the same dang time! Coming over here after I caught her with my man. I was just too weak to talk. I balled up my fists, and watched both of the girls walk towards me.

"Erica. I just wanted to check on you, while you're down. Here is a get well soon card," Ashley said, hugging me and giving me the card.

She was so sweet.

"I wanted to check on you too. I don't know you, but I wanted you to know that I'm a real woman, and I do care about your feelings. Men are dogs, girl. I got six kids. My man did me wrong, and I left him," Crystal told me.

She handed me some beautiful roses, and gave me a hug. I had tears in my eyes. I instantly forgave Crystal. She showed me more love than Joe did, and she didn't even know me!

"Heeeeeeeeey, honey!" Kenya PimpCity Brown screamed, running in my room, like she won the lottery.

She gave me a big, juicy, best friend kiss on the forehead.

"I love you girl!" Kenya said hugging me and handing me my favorite, a fruit basket.

"How's my girl?' Uncle Chicago said. He was looking serious, but concerned.

"Aunty, aunty!" my niece, Bre'Shauna yelled.

"Hey cuz. I flew down from Colorado when I heard," my cousin Santana said.

Then, two cool, nice looking dudes came in. Ohhh! My boys showed me love.

"You aiight?" Mr. Pimp City (Candler Road; Decatur King) said.

He was with his six-foot-four, light-skinned, Blood, gangsta homie, who was from the Dominican Republic. His name was Trapp.

"Erica, heal up." Trapp said, in a cool, Snoop Dog voice.

"Baby, hold on. Hold on. Let me get to my baby. I want all of yall to pray for my baby with me. Pray that that African man don't kill her! He stressing her out!" my mom said.

That did it. The tears began to rush out of my brown eyes. I was holding back too much pain.

"Good, God! Joyce, Kenya, Erica. Lord, let's pray for the child." Rev. Bobby Brown, my pastor, and his wife, Hannah came in.

Then my cousin, Porsche showed up. I hadn't seen Porsche in ten years! She was still beautiful! She had been in Cobb County for years.

This was just too much.

My mom held one hand. Evangelist Hannah, held my other hand.

Rev. Bobby Brown prayed, "Dear Father, we all ask for forgiveness. You, Lord, are the King of Kings. By your stripes, we are healed. Whatever we bind here on earth, you will bind in heaven. Lose her! Set her free! Heal her! In Jesus mighty name, Amen!"

Reverend Bobby Brown prayed strong, anointed, and loud.

I cried. Everyone said Amen.

"It'll be alright," mama said.

"Yea, Aunty, I love you. Ima sing you a song," Bre'Shauna said.

Bre'Shauna sounded like a young Alicia Keys. She sung 'Amazing Grace.'

My visitors stayed with me, and we all laughed, talked, and reminisced for an hour. Then everyone left. Kenya stayed back.

"We need to talk, boo."

"What?" I asked, finally getting a word out of my mouth.

"The 12 came to my door this morning."

"Who is 12?" I asked.

"That's what the inmates call the police."

"Oh, girl, sorry. What they say?" I asked.

"That I was wanted for murder."

"What??!!!" I felt like I swallowed an ironing board, and a skate board at the same dang time.

I know that if they wanted her, they wanted me too. Precious probably died.

"So, what should I do?" Kenya asked.

"I don't . . ."

"Freeze! Police! Kenya Brown, you have the right to remain silent. Anything you say or do, can be held against you in a court of law."

"Miss Brown, you're in trouble too." the female officer said.

What else could go wrong? I'm in a hospital bed, hurting, pregnant, heartbroken, and going to jail for murder?!

I just stared at the dark chocolate female officer.

"Listen, I'm Officer Walker. This is very serious," she said, trying to show off her nice figure and cute face. She looked innocent, like we coulda been smoking and drinking partners.

Then she slammed Kenya face down, on the floor, right there in my hospital room!

NO MORE PIMPIN'

I watched them take Kenya away. She didn't even fight or shed a tear. There comes a time in your life, when you know it's over. You know you have no win.

She was tired of running. Everything she had done, had fallen back on her; hard.

Now I'm laying here thinking, hurting, stressing, and crying.

"Miss Brown, do you know anything about the brutal murder of Precious McCledon?" Detective Walker asked.

"No."

"That's a bold faced lie, do you want another try?" the chocolate female detective asked.

"No. I want my lawyer."

"Perfect. Your lawyer will wait for you, because we have you on camera chopping this slut up like Freddie vs. Jason! You stupid, young, pregnant, dumb, hot pussy, whore. I should lock you up, and beat the living shit out of you!"

"Erica Brown, you are a dumb slut. You are under arrest for murder. What kind of slutty, low-life, inconsiderate mother are you? You are the reason why black kids ain't shit!"

"Damn, Erica Brown. You are going down!" the black detective yelled.

Twah.

I spit in her face!

Smack! Smack! Crack!

She hit me with her stick.

I kicked her in the eyes.

Smack!

She punched me with the handcuffs.

Wam!

I elbowed her in the chest. Then, I took her handcuffs off, and cuffed her to the bed. I had all my energy back now!

Next, I snatched off her police uniform.

"Wooo. Nice body. Hot for a cop. You shoulda been a stripper at Magic City," I told the young cop.

She had on a tiny red bikini, with the bra to match. The bra had black stars on the nipples.

She was trying to snatch her wrists off!

Smack!

"Pop that couchie," I joked, smacking the cop on her hot ass.

"Erica! Erica!"

"Yeah?"

"Wake up," Kenya said.

I rubbed my eyes, actually happy that this was just a dream. Kenya didn't really go to jail. I wasn't wanted.

"Come on!" Kenya yelled, grabbing my hands. She snatched me off the hospital bed.

Now, I'm holding Kenya's hand, flying through the hospital hall, like the female James Bond!

"Excuse me. Pardon me. My bad," I said to a nurse, then to a man in a wheelchair, which nearly crashed when I accidentally kicked him, while I was running in my white and blue hospital gown.

My nipples were hard, and hanging out of my gown. They were considered perfect. Not too big, and not too small. But they were jiggling baby!

"Hey!" a man yelled.

"Oops, my bad," I said, knocking his coffee out of his hand.

I had no idea where we were running to. Maybe my dream had come true. Maybe Kenya knew, and we were running from the police!

Oh, God. Two fine chicks on the run. Wooh. I felt the cold air whistling on my soft booty.

"What, nigga?! Yea, you thought she was still sick, didn't you Joe?" Kenya asked.

Joe was standing there holding his baby, and eating Micky D's with his two black-eyed having baby mama.

"Look, Erica. I can explain."

"Save it, Joe. You know I'm sick, but you still sitting here with this beat up slut and this tank head ass baby. He too black to be yours. What you need to do, is get a blood test." I said.

"Ok, I will get a blood test soon," Joe said.

"Naw, nigga. You getting a blood test now!" Kenya yelled.

"Ouch! Crazy slut!" Joe yelled, jumping back.

Wow, Kenya is crazy! She just cut the nigga arm, and put some of his blood on his napkin.

"I will do the damn blood test myself if you don't get your dog ass up," Kenya told him.

"Ok. Ok. Damn."

"Leave the slut," Kenya said.

"Naw, she can go," I said.

We drove to the courthouse, and set everything up. Joe just kept looking at Kenya real crazy!

'When I move, you move; just like that . . . . stand up . . . stand up . . .'

The old Luda song, blasted from Luda's burnt orange Cutlass Supreme. Old school, with a delicious, gleaming, clean pain job.

Then we all get out of my sparkling, candy apple red, sticky glossed up, Maybach that I took from Joe's ass! Joe was still giving Kenya that look; like he was thinking, this slut is psycho!

We walked up to the courthouse of downtown Atlanta; the home of M.L.K., Monica, T.I., and Ludacris.

Beeeep!

"Damn, why dis beep shit going off?" I asked when I walked through the metal detector.

"Oh, mam, remove your bling, bling," Miss Yorker said.

"Oh, yeah, of course. I been wearing this platinum for so long, it's part of my skin."

I removed my two thousand dollar necklace, and my seventy-five thousand dollar watch.

Beeeep! It went off again.

"Mam, make sure anything that seems metal is removed," some smart ass po-po in uniform said.

"Hold up, partna. You a little too close to my lady," Joe said, staring the six foot-seven guy up and down.

Even though Joe was only six feet, one-hundred seventy five pounds, he didn't play the radio when it came to me. Anyone fuck with me, Joe will blow.

"Excuse me fella, but miss, please step to the side," the man said to Joe like a chump. Then, he pushed me.

"Get your hands off of me!"

Bam. Bam

Two punches. A blow to the head, and a super upper cut to the chin.

Beeep! Beep! Beep!

Joe sent him sliding through the metal detector.

"Now you remove your metal, sucker!" I said, laughing hella hard.

The dude slid through the metal detector on his back. Now he was knocked out sleep like a female dinosaur on Friday night!

"Well, I guess yall can go through the metal detector now, since my supervisor got KNOCKED THE FUCK OUT!" the brown, stripper looking, baby faced, Miss Yorker said.

We all laughed.

"Thanks Miss Yorker," I said, looking at the brown skinned officer's name tag.

We talked to this white lady named Mickens. She scheduled the appointment for the blood test.

"Can I ask you a question, Mr. Brown?" Miss Mickens asked.

"What up?"

"Erica is beautiful. Why wouldn't you claim the baby?"

"Who said I wasn't claiming that baby? It's my other baby," Joe explained.

"Men," she said, shaking her head while filling out the paperwork.

When she was finished, we all got up and left. The blood test would be Friday.

"Hold up, gotta pee," Joe said, running back inside.

Me, Kenya, Munchie, and her baby, all walked to our cars.

"Damn, you sexy as hell for a white girl. And you got a black girl booty!" Joe told Miss Mickens.

She smiled, shook her head, and cleared her throat.

"Don't you already have a bad case of double baby mama drama?"

"Ha, ha. Fuck that! You look like a white Halle Berry!"

Smack! I hit him across the head with her folders.

"You look like a human dog!"

"Chill out," Kenya told me, pulling me back.

"Let's go, girl. That nigga will get what he deserve," Kenya said, walking me to the door.

I was crying and angry. Now he wants a white girl with a big butt!

I laughed to myself, but I was mad at the same dang time. This nigga is a super dog! I'm so sick of this African! I'm sending him back on the first boat; him and that damn monkey that Whitney got!

I BEE'S IN DA TRAP

Joe was chillin in the projects on Glenwood Road, in Decatur. He was sitting on the black leather couch, counting money.

"That's 20 bricks," the tall light skinned Blood, they called Trapp, said. Trapp stood six-foot-four inches, had a low cut, and was Dominican, though he looked mixed.

Trapp was carrying a black Gucci bag. He opened up, and dropped the twenty-five bricks of snowflakes on the floor, right in front of Joe's leg.

"Suwooo," Yae screamed, coming out of the kitchen with a blunt in her hand. Yae had on all black, with her red bandana. She was smooth, and dark skinned. She represented the Blood Gang harder than any female I know.

"Bet. Trapp, count the money. It's all there, dog," Joe said.

Yae just blew smoke out of her mouth, and rubbed her red 9mm, while she watched the two Nine Tre Gangstas.

Trapp gave them an evil smile, and counted the money.

Bam!

For some reason, Trapp threw all the money on the glass table.

Crack!

The champaign glass broke.

Trapp pulled out two red glock nines, and started shooting toward Joe, too fast for Joe to react.

Boom. Boom. Boom. Boom.

He fell down. Two shots in the chest, two in the face. Yae quickly shot at the same time, hitting dude in the back of the head, twice. His head looked like a red strawberry, melted in ice-cream.

Blood was everywhere! Joe lay motionless on the red carpet floor.

Sling! Yae cut the nigga head off with a sword.

"Burn it," Trapp told her.

Then Joe stood up.

"Thanks Dog. That was a close call."

"All day, every day. Blood love."

"Now back to business," Trapp responded. He picked the racks of money up, and counted it.

"Four-hundred-thousand on da dot. Got to be more careful."

Pow! Then he shot the dude again.

"You're right. Everyone that smiles in your face ain't your friend," Joe said, staring at his headless best friend. He was one of Joe's closest friends in high school.

When Trapp was counting the money, Trey reached for his gun to shoot Trapp, but Trapp quickly responded, and beat the dude to the punch. Now, he was dead, with no head!

Yae tossed the head outside to Joe's laughing hyena. The hyena's jaw is one of the most powerful jaws on Earth. A hyena could chew and crush a human skull with his jaws. Even though hyenas are wild, African, cannibalistic animals, they were once house pets in ancient Egypt. Joe had a powerful, mean, spotted purring hyena.

"Hey, Trapp," I said, speaking to the cool killa.

"What's poppin, Foxy Red?" Trapp replied. He gave me that look. I shook it off, and gave Joe a hug.

WAP!

He slapped the spit outta me!

"Slut! You want to fuck Trapp?! Slut, Ima kill you!" Joe yelled at me.

He hit me so hard, two of my teeth came out. My mouth was bleeding like a river runs. I was embarrassed and hurt. The shame I felt was worse than the pain. Why did this stupid nigga hit me in front of this girl and his homeboy?

"Slut, get out," Joe said. He grabbed me by my arm, and slung me into the door.

Boom.

I heard my arm break! Damn, that shit hurt!

"Get out, before I kill you!" Joe yelled.

I was on the porch, on my knees staring up at him. My arm was bent backwards like an entire football team had tackled me!

Pow! He fired, shooting in the air. I was scared as hell!

"Chill, dog," Trapp said.

Joe just looked at Trapp.

Man, I cried. Yae picked me up.

"I called the ambulance," Ashley yelled. She had followed me there. We were going to get our nails done. Ashley had just won five-hundred-thousand from the lottery, so she was paying. She didn't realize what Joe did to me, until he shot his gun.

"Come on. Help me carry her," Yae said.

Trapp picked me up in his arms, laid me down on his back seat, and drove off in his red Hummer.

Ashley, Kenya, and my mom were at the hospital.

"My baby! Did I lose my baby?" I asked while crying and shaking. I was worried.

"No dear," the RN, Miss Bailey, told me.

"We been praying hard," mom said.

"Yes, prayer works Miss Brown. Your daughter's arm was broken, but the baby is healthy," the RN said.

ON THE RUN

"Enough is enough," mom said.

"Stay with me, girl. He don't know me," Porsche said.

"Naw, I don't want to leave GA."

"Well, I'll rent you a room at the Lodge in Marietta. He'll never come there," Ashley said.

"Hello?" I said, answering my phone.

"How my baby doing?" Kenya asked.

"Terrible, girl" I answered, honestly.

"It will be alright. Where you at?" Kenya asked, while smoking on some Keysha.

"Guuuurl, on the side of the expressway, tryna find somewhere to stay," I told my girl.

"Really? Fuck Joe, stay with me. I'll cut that nigga up, and throw him in the trash can," Kenya told me.

"I guess. I'll let you know," I told her.

Joe kissed Kenya. He was sitting on the couch with her the whole time. Kenya had on some skin tight boy shorts, and a white wife beater. She was giggling, and pushing Joe off of her. He picked her up, and laid her on the floor.

"Joe, Joe. Aww. Shit. You feel so good, so hard, so strong," Kenya said, as he was lying on top of her, kissing her neck, massaging her back, squeezing her booty, tonguing her ear, and pulling her hair. Joe wanted Kenya badly, and truth be told, Kenya wanted that Junglewood!

The fucked up part is, Kenya never hung up! I just muted my phone, and listened, stunned.

The whole truck was on pause. My mom, Ashley, and Porsche all held their mouths wide open like a prostitute on a Friday night, in July, on Metropolitan.

"I got an idea," I said with the phone on mute. We all sat on the side of the busy expressway, at four o'clock PM, Friday, the 13th.

I dialed the number . . .

Great! She picked up.

"Hello?"

"Mute your phone," I told Daja.

"Ahh, Ahh. Fuck me, Joe. Beat it, beat it, beat it, ahh. I'm wet, I'm wet. I'm cummin' daddy. Fuck this pussy! Give it to me daddy!"

Butt smacking.

Joe had her on her knees, on the living room carpet. Beating it, pounding it, fast. He pulled out, and went in her mouth. He began to shake and explode as he held her head.

She swallowed the milkshake and played in her pussy with two fingers. She began to explode, and hopped on top of his face. He held her ass, and licked every inch of her butt and pussy.

I hung up.

Everybody looked at me. I shook my head. I was speechless.

Mom drove.

"Damn, that's fucked up," Daja said, calling me back.

"Yea," I said, extremely hurt.

Not so much because of Joe. I expect a nigga to cheat, but not Kenya. I was hurt, disappointed, and shocked. I stared out of the window and watched the cars zooming past, and the trees on the expressway. I cried. Kenya was the only friend I thought I really had. Now, I'm with Ashley, who I just met, and Porsche, who I ain't seen in years!

Who can I trust? No one, these days.

I stayed hidden in Marietta for ten months. I got bigger and bigger as the months went by. I didn't call Kenya, or Joe. I never answered my phone, unless it was mom, Porsche, or Ashley calling me.

I got me a job at a prison, in Cobb County. Crenshaw State Prison.

Mom, Porsche, and Ashley were the only people who knew where I was. I didn't even bother to call Daja, even though Daja was cool as ice-cream in July; no lie.

No matter what, blood is thicker than water. Just like Joe told the cops to lock Daja up, then turned around and beat up all the cops up for shooting her. He's still her brother.

I was riding the bus for the first time in my life. Standing at the bus stop, nine months pregnant. Things had changed in my life, for the best. Ashley and I worked at the prison. We became close friends.

I was going to a new church, every Wednesday and Saturday. A Seven day Adventist, Baptist church. It was called the Ray of Hope International Ministry. Evangelist Hannah Jeannette Shepherd, Minister Joshua Levi Brown, and Apostle Rutherford lead the church.

This was such a great church. The choir director had a weird name, Stozzi. She was sweet though.

I was also in college. South Cobb Christian College.

I was standing at the bus stop, feeling as fat as an elephant who was pregnant with twins. My white Air Force Ones felt like bricks! I missed my Maybach. Joe was the only normal nigga in the world that could crash a red Maybach, buy another Maybach the same day, then give the car to me!

But, I was too proud to go get it. I never wanted to look at Joe again.

Now, I was standing at the bus stop on Cobb Parkway.

"Dang!" It started raining and I didn't bring a rain coat or an umbrella, brella, brella. Hey!

The sky was dark as Griffin Georgia, at midnight, with no street lights on, even though it was four in the afternoon.

Booooom! Boooom!

The thunder and lightning was as loud as a rocket on steroids!

"Lord, where is the bus?"

I saw it, thank God. This busy street was empty as a cowboy ghost town, except for the three cars at the BP gas station, across the street.

The bus pulled up. Yes! I quickly stepped on.

"Oooh!"

Bam!

I slipped on the first step and fell down. I hit my head, hard.

"Hey! Help her!" I heard an old black lady yell.

"I got her," a big black guy said. He had to be Muslim, 'cause he had on the hat.

I woke up in the hospital for the thirteenth time!

"Hey, cutie, you bout to have a baby", the big guy said.

I just looked at him.

"My name is Worm. Do you want me to call anyone? I was waiting for you to wake up. Your iPhone cracked."

I was in excruciating pain. I could hear the three-hundred pound cool Worm, but his words sounded like we were in the ocean talking to fish.

"Ahhhhh! Shiiiittt! Help me!" I screamed from the bottom of my pretty toes!

The nurses ran in, right past the six-feet-five-inch Big Worm.

"Hook it up! Grab her hands. Hold her legs. Push. Push. She's coming out. She's coming. Push!" I heard the doctor and nurses say.

"Ahhh! Fuck this! Hell! Hell! Hell! Ahhh! Ahh! Joe! Joe! Get your ass over here, Joe!" I cried and yelled. I actually saw Joe, standing at the edge of the bed, hugging my ex-friend Kenya, and laughing at me.

"Just push the baby out, so we can go fuck!" Joe yelled.

"Yea, Erica. Joe got some good wood! Push that nappy-headed, ugly ass baby out, biiiitch!!" Kenya laughed.

"Nooooo! Fuck you! Fuck you, Joe! Kenya! I hate you! Help! Somebody help me!" I was hysterical.

"Stop kicking, Miss Brown. Hold her legs, mister," Doctor Harper said.

Crying . . .

The baby. Awww. She was beautiful.

"Give me my baby!" I yelled.

"Aww, my grandbaby! My first grandbaby!" my mom said, appearing out of nowhere.

Snap. Snap.

Ashley was taking pictures of me holding my baby. Then, she took pictures of my mom holding my baby. She came out crying, so I named her Crymeka Beyoncé Brown.

"Let me hold her," my brother Dontae said.

"She is so, so pretty, with all that hair," Porsche said.

"Where is Kenya and Joe! Don't! No! Don't let him hold my baby!"
I yelled when Joe picked her up.

"Hell no! You dog! You ruined my life!" I yelled at Joe.

"Calm down."

"Fuck you, Kenya! Die, you two-faced slut! Ima kill you!" I shouted
at Kenya, as I jumped out of the hospital bed.

Bang!

"Ooouuch!"

I fell back on the bed, hitting the plate of cold steak and rice with
my elbow.

"Erica, that's your brother, Dontae, and your cousin, Porsche. Kenya
and Joe ain't here," Ashley told me.

I started turning my head from side to side. I was tripping. My long
hair was a mess. I looked like I just fucked a baboon! I felt like I got
fucked by a silver back gorilla with a horse dick!

I looked at my mom. A small tear was slowly sliding down her face.
I started crying. Her daughter was losing it. This man had driven me
crazy!

POP DAT CAT

'Bandz to Make Her Dance' by Juicy J was blasting from the speakers of the Pimp City Strip Club.

"Damn, that ass clapping," Joe said, standing at the stage, while Lil Wayne spit on the Juicy J track.

"2 chains!" Joe yelled, as he put ten brand new hundred dollar bills inside her crack. She stood on her knees, clapping her butt in Joe's face at the end of the stage.

Joe felt his phone vibrate. He froze.

"Damn!" Joe ran to outside the club. Skittles can wait, he said to himself. A tall female with a Jamaican accent walked towards Joe.

"What up, bro?" Danie asked as he flew past her, out the door.

"Nothing." Joe said.

Joe stood outside the club. Maybe he did feel a little guilty. His childhood sweetheart was having his baby, while he was tricking off at the strip club!

"Damn!" Joe cursed again.

"Hello?" Joe's female spy said.

"Where she at?"

"Cobb Medical."

"What she have?"

"Baby girl. Seven pounds, two ounces."

THIS GIRL IS ON FIRE!

Joe turned on the old, slow, sexy song by Miguel, 'Adorn You.' He jumped in his second, candy apply red Maybach that he had once given me.

I was walking out of the hospital with my baby and family when I heard my song; the song that Joe and I made love to for two days straight. The song that we made this baby to.

I smiled. It brought back memories when I heard Miguel blasting from the fifteen inch speakers. Look at my car; still spankin', sparklin' new. The apple red was gleaming hard in the Georgia sun. I guess he did care. He found me!

I did feel a little better now, but who told him?

He stopped in front of me and our new baby. My mom, cousin, family and friends stared at the car, watching the dark black tinted windows roll down.

"What the?" I was so hurt, I almost dropped my baby.

This nigga had another chick driving my car, to come and see me and my baby.

"No he didn't!"

She had on the twenty thousand dollar necklace my cousin Santana bought me!

"Hold the baby," I said, giving her to Dontae.

Too late.

Ashley grabbed the girl by the top of her hair, and tried to snatch her butt out the window. The car was rolling backwards. Ashley was running backwards, with the girl's body half was out the car.

BANG!

She hit the concrete like an egg.

"Boot time!" I yelled.

Then, Porsche, Ashley and I stomped her.

The police pulled up. Joe grabbed the baby.

The cops ran up on us.

"Take a picture," ignorant Joe said.

He had the bold lion face nerves to pose for a damn picture with my baby, while he boldly disrespected me!

Snap!

My scary ass brother Dontae took the picture!

Bam!

"Whoa."

Joe stumbled backwards and fell down on the curve the second he gave my mom the baby.

To my surprise, my brother knocked the shit outta him! After Joe handed Crymeka to mama, he ran up on him, and punched him!

"No, Dontae!" I yelled, 'cause the cops were here.

"Stop son!" mom yelled.

Dontae went crazy. Kicking him.

"Nigga, you!"

Bam!

"Hit!"

Bam!

"My sister!"

Bam!

"Again!"

Bam!

"Ima kill you!"

Bam! Boom. A gun fired.

"Freeze!" three white cops said.

We were all shocked. I was dinosaur stiff! Joe shot my brother!

"No! No! Son! My baby!" my mom went ballistic!

My mom went off! She was going nuts, man. Mom gave Crymeka to Ashley, dived on her son, and cried while holding and shaking him.

"Please maam," the white female cop said.

This was the first time in my life that I ever saw my mom on her knees. She never cried this hard. This was her seventeen year old baby boy!

Everyone, the family, the cops, and all the people outside the hospital just stared at my mom and my bloody brother as he lay on the street in front of the hospital.

"I hate you! I hate you! You dog! You shot my baby!" my mom cried, rocking Dontae, and holding the top of his neck. She reminded me of Jada Pinkett-Smith, in the hit movie, Set It Off.

I was about to set this ish off! My little brother . . .

"Dontae!"

Kah Boom!

Two female cops slammed me, and then handcuffed me.

"Hey, let her go!" Porsche yelled.

"Miss, calm down," a blonde cop told her.

Twah!

Porsche spit in her face.

"That's my cousin, trick!"

Bam. Bam. Boom.

Porsche punched the white cop in her nose.

Two cops tackled her to the ground, and even though they rushed her from the back, it wasn't easy.

She had one girl in a headlock, but the other red-headed cop hit Porsche with her baton. Then, a huge white muscle cop slapped the cuffs on my bloody-headed cousin.

"Get off her, you fuck man!" I yelled, while they slung me in the back seat, like a thief!

Two huge, white, cops who looked like wrestlers handcuffed Joe with ease. Dontae had put a pretty good beat down on Joe, catching him off guard! Joe was still stunned!

Ashley and my mom were with my brother on the ambulance. I think Ashley liked my brother. Oh well.

Now, I was about to lose my brother, and my new job, twenty-four hours after the birth of my daughter. AND, I'm going to jail at the same dang time! Hell, I might lose my baby behind this too!

At least my girl Ashley didn't go to jail.

"Hey! You with the black leggings, and long Indian hair. Come 'ere!" the red-headed female cop yelled at Ashley.

"What? I'm with my people, dog!" Ashley responded.

She was climbing in the back of the ambulance.

Bre'Shauna and uncle Chi came. Bre'Shauna was holding my daughter, and rocking her. Her ten year old, handsome, white, adopted brother, Tear Drop, was tickling my baby's toes. Bre'Shauna and Tear Drop were two adorable kids.

"Awww, how cute," Bre'Shauna's dad, Roscoe said.

Ahhh, shitty, titty! It's about to be trouble! I could smell it, like funky, crack couchie! Roscoe was BMF, the notorious Black Mob Family. Something was going to happen. Like Bat Man in a red suit!

I felt it in my now flat stomach! I was as lucky as a stripper that had a birthday on a Friday! I was proud of my flat stomach. No stretch marks! Heeey!

"Maam, what's your name?" the white female officer who was driving the police car said.

"Eat a dick!" I yelled.

"I eat one every night, nigger," the smart needle lip blonde said, looking at me in the rearview mirror.

"Oh, yeah, biiietch? Take off these cuffs, and I'll show you what this nigga can do! I'll beat the white off your pale, funny, freckle face ass!"

Bang!

I kicked the cage that separated the front seat from the back.

"Well, I'm about to show you what this pale face cracker can do. I'm about to take your black ass to jail! You nigger, Nicki Minaj wanna be! You in the wrong neck of the woods, nigger slut! You're going to jail in Cobb County!" she bragged.

Bang. Bang. Bang. Boom. Crash.

"Wow!" is all I could say from my 'spaceships in the projects' shock!

Two huge, black Dooly trucks smashed into the police car. One from the front left side, and one from the right side. We were at the red light. The trucks came out of nowhere, at a very high speed, breaking big mouth's neck; killing her on impact.

Smash. Click. Boom.

Roscoe, my big brother opened the door. I knew he would be trouble.

"Mob Shit!" big bro, Roscoe yelled.

"Straight up!" my cousin Santana said, standing in the middle of the busy street with a terminator chopper.

"Is the slut dead?" his big homie, Dirty, asked.

"Yea. Slut double dead," Summer Hill, A.K.A., John said.

The MOB was on point!

Boom. Boom. Bang. Crash.

Fire . . . Smoke . . .

A police car flipped and slid down the sidewalk.

Bang! It crashed through the bus stop. Then the police car started sliding down the sidewalk, upside-down going forty miles an hour!

Boom!

It hit a pole and stopped.

I saw a huge eighteen wheeler truck appear like a transformer!

"Blatt! Blatt! Suwooo!" Trapp yelled.

Bloods had arrived too!

I had the Bloods and the MOB rescuing me at the same dang time!

Trapp had rammed the police car that was transporting Joe, off of the road. The car was on fire, while it sat upside-down.

Trapp and Skooter just stared at me and smiled.

"Red Rubies bark at yo dog" Trapp told the female Bloods.

Brittany, A.K.A., Bubblegum, Yae, and Lola B hopped out the truck and ran to check on Joe.

"Pull him out!" Bubblegum yelled.

The three girls saved that piece of dog, dirt, baby daddy of mine. Oh, Lord. Why did he have to be a dog?! All dogs have their day, but this nigga won't die!

Joe was dragged out of the window by one of the Blood girls. He got up and looked at me. Then he stood on the sidewalk, dusted his pants off, winked his eye at me, and smiled.

"I hate you!" I yelled, while charging at him.

"Chill," San told me, holding me back while I was swinging at him and crying.

I was kicking at the air, as Santana pulled me into the Dooley truck and drove off.

"Not now. No more hot shit. This is Cobb County. He will pay later." San told me.

"Burn the car. Erase Joe and Erica's fingerprints," Bubblegum told her cousin, Lola B.

"Fo sho," she replied, pouring gas, and striking the match.

Boom. Flames. Dark Smoke. Boom.

Yae blew up the cop car that I was in. No fingerprints.

Kah-boo yah! KAHBOOOM! Whoa!!

Dressed in all black, out of nowhere, Kenya PimpCity Brown fired a flame thrower, and destroyed all four tires on the police car.

Crash! Bang!

The car slammed into a pink panther minivan.

"Get her out, Devin!" Kenya told her sis.

Bang!

Devin the Doll, kicked the front windshield out of the police car with her stilettos.

"Got a gummy bear?" Porsche asked, after she crawled out of the police car backwards, in her black mini skirt and knee high boots.

Devin shot the handcuffs off of her.

"Naw, but I got a milk shake and a blunt!" Devin said, laughing.

"Hell, naw!" Porsche said, grabbing the blunt and the strawberry milkshake.

What about the witnesses at the hospital? Oh well, I thought.

I had enough to worry about. I listened to the song by Alicia Keys, 'This Girl is on Fire!' as I watched the cop cars erupt into huge, hot, exploding flames. I was really on my hot girl shit. THIS girl was on fire!

FACE BOOKING

I was riding in the big boy truck with San, feeling drunk and high, and I ain't smoked or drank a dang thing! I decided to whip out my phone and update my status on Facebook.

Erica Hustle-n-Flow Brown
You can give people your all, but they will run over you, complain and use you, and STILL WANT MORE!!! Wtf? Lol.   79 likes 8 comments

Mr. Pimp City
True. Real Talk, cause you know I look out for my whole hood, and you can never give too much.   2 likes

Cheetara P.
Girl, you always on point!

Keke
That's the shit I don't like!

> **Vanilla Bean**
> Guuurl, for super real!

Kenyatta
For real girl. Mother fuckers up here in Chicago be on some bull!
                                                          3 likes

Erica Hustle-n-Flow Brown
Lol. That's a good one Kenyatta, mother fuckers in Chicago be on some bull! Lmao. Talkin bout like the Chicago Bulls? Lol.

Ivory
So, so true.

Janise

I'm so tired of not being appreciated. Diamond and Crystal is so damn silly, girl we were about to come surprise you with a huge chocolate, gummy bear, ice-cream cake! Lmao.   2 likes

Erica Hustle-n-Flow Brown

Lmao. Wow. Sounds good. Kinky and silly. But good! ☺

"Erica!" my mom yelled into the phone, knocking Facebook off my cracked iPhone. I would have to get another one soon.

"Yes mom."

"Dontae is fine baby. He should leave tomorrow."

"Mom, I'm right behind you."

"What? You scared the apple out of me!" mom joked when she jumped.

"Ha, ha. Funny mama. Hey Dontae. I love you," I said hugging my brother's neck really tight. He had gotten shot in both of his legs, with a 9mm, but by the grace of God, he would be fine. My brother stopped smiling. The huge, red, Kool-Aid smile disappeared like slavery!

"Awwe. That cute little brother will be fine, until I beat his mother fucking ass, head up, you fuck nigga!" Joe said.

Immediately, I stood up.

Bam! Bam! Bam!

I went crazy, punching him like a wild woman.

Bam!

Shit. One punch from Joe knocked me over my brother's bed. Boom! Then on the floor.

Bam!

Santana punched him.

Woosh! He punched San.

"I'll kill you San. You, Joyce, the baby, this slut, and this slut ass nigga on this hospital bed," Joe barked.

San just stared in Joe's eyes. Joe had two fine ass strippers with him. This nigga had balls bigger than China! I know San was gonna kill him. I just didn't know when.

Pow. Pow. Gunfire; in the hospital!

Joe fired in the ceiling, but we all knew that Joe is a killer too. The nurses and doctors ran into the room.

"What is . . ."

"Nothing. My wife fell. Vanilla, you ok? Shawty Rock, let's go." Joe said to his beautiful, yellow girl, and his brown cutie.

I fought my way up, and walked out of the room behind him. I walked fast, like Jason in the woods. I didn't care anymore. I would rather go to jail, play spades and eat Ramen noodles all day, than to be humiliated any further by this man. I was about to kill him. I'd had enough. I was getting closer to him.

Dam!

The elevator closed right in my face. Joe and his two girls laughed at me.

Ima get the last laugh mother fucker! I ran down the stairs. San had given me his gun.

Blong!

I burst out the door! He was tongue kissing both of his girls at the same dang time! Oh no! Hot grits in Hell! He dying today!

Pow!

"Ouch! Ouch! God. God, No. What, what, what is wrong with you?"

"Shut up. I'll kill you slut."

Twah.

Joe spit in my face, after he surprised me, and shot me in my leg.

I was in pain. His hoes just laughed at me, and drove off in my Maybach! All these damn people just looked at me, and kept walking.

"Hey sweetie, let me help you up," a correctional officer named Miss Jackson said.

"Hey. That's Miss Brown from the prison. You ok, girl?" Miss Lang said.

The two cool females helped me into the emergency room. I got a room right next to my brother. I gave up, and went straight to sleep.

"Dear Father. Bless Erica Brown. She needs you. She loves you. Lord, save her and forgive her for her sins. I pray that you bless her and her child, her mom, her brothers, and her sisters. Lord, you know what we need on earth. You see everything. Lord, bless your child. In Jesus name we pray, Amen." Evangelist Hannah Sheppard prayed.

I was so excited. Rachael, from TBIV TV station, my beautiful chocolate beautician, Liz, and sister Cedra and her husband John were there. My church members were all by my bedside praying. Rev. Bobby Brown was dressed like a chocolate prince! He was wearing a purple, silk suit. His curls were so wet and wacky, it made me wiggle and giggle.

A nurse who looked like Halle Berry walked in my room singing, 'Girl on Fire,' by Alicia Keys.

"How you doing, hun?"

"I'm ok. Blessed, Miss . . .?" I said, not knowing her name.

"Oh, Miss Yorker. I'm your nurse, hun. If you need me, push this button." Miss Yorker said, as she walked away.

Not trying to sound gay, but she had a dynamic booty for a nurse!

"Well sweetheart, you have to start coming back to church", Evangelist Sheppard said.

She always encouraged me. My life was flashing before my eyes. I was being run down by a freight train. I felt like the chocolate Tarzan, swinging from tree to tree, in the damn jungle.

"What the hell?" I wondered when I saw the tall, brown, gorgeous Officer Jackson walk in my room.

She whispered in my ear. "I got your gun, girl. Be safe."

"Oh. Thanks, baby." I smiled.

"Here, you might need it, girl. Bust his ass!" Miss Jackson whispered to me while laughing, and slipping me the red .38 special.

Yeeeaaah!!!! My favorite lady in the world, Joyce walked into my room! She had my baby, and what? Wow.

"Long time no see," Daja said.

She gave me a hug, and a kiss on my right cheek.

I reached for my baby, Crymeka. Mom handed her to me.

"What you been doing, girl?" I asked.

"Oh, trick, I been back in Seattle, chillin' wit my fam."

"Ha, ha. What's going on up there, sugar foot?" I joked, playing with Crymeka's feet.

"Nothing gurrl. Same ole' thang. Love you. Sorry about having the worst brother in the world," Daja said, now staring down at me, looking serious.

"I . . ." I started, but didn't have anything good to say.

She squeezed my hand.

"Erica, I love you like a sister. I'm here for you. I hate that my brother is turning into such a bad person."

I never saw Daja cry. She was a very strong woman; tough like her brother, and beautiful. Her eyes were filled with water, like a bath tub, filled to the top, about to run over.

Crymeka started to get fussy, so mama picked her up and rocked her while we talked.

"This is messing up our friendship. I can't really choose sides. But no girl should be hurt. Erica, I love you. I'm going back to Seattle with my fiancé. We getting married in the ATL! You better heal up, and come! The wedding is on Saturday, the 4th out July, at the always crunk, Ray of Hope, with Minister Joshua Levi Brown! Be there, girl!" Daja said to me, now getting excited.

I was happy for her. I've known her all my life. She and Joe had different dads. Joe's dad was a cool, chocolate chip African named Harold Render. Daja's dad was a street nigga named Turf. He moved kilos from Seattle to Miami, New Jersey, Connecticut, Decatur, IL, to ATL. Turf was not a smurf!

Turf was the man. He had a fifteen bedroom castle in Seattle, WA, that Daja loved going to. It had a huge playground, roller coasters, other rides, and a pool. Daja was always traveling back and forth from Seattle to Atlanta.

"I'm so glad you and Champ getting married." I said. I was happy for her, but a little envious, since it wasn't me.

I glanced at the TV. I was watching Family Hustle. I loved T.I., my ATL homie, and Tiny, the ride or die chick of the decade!

I was also reading T.I.'s new book, Trouble & Triumph: A Novel of Power & Beauty.

Champ had on a nice, black, Polo suit. He was a professional, light weight boxer from Athens, GA.

"Here's my book of poems. Read this, and you will cheer up. Inspirational Water for Christian Mothers," Champ told me, giving me a beautiful copy of his inspirational book of poems. He was saved, and strong at the same time.

Could I ever find a saved man with swag? Someone like my preaching cousin, Joshua. Minister Joshua Levi Brown, was an ex thug;

a drug dealing prisoner, pimp, and a Blood, who turned into a fire, swagged out preacher! Maybe God would bless me.

I continued to talk with everyone until they left. My uncle, O.G. Hood and Dog Man were there too. They had just gotten out of Phillips Prison.

I needed a change. I watched Love and Hip Hop-Decatur, and realized I needed Jesus. I needed God. I was tired.

"Give me my baby back." I told my mom. Everyone had left except my mom and beautiful baby, Crymeka.

She was adorable!

A week later, I was riding to church, listening to Big Pimpin', Jay Z, and UGK. Ashley was driving her fly ride because I was on crutches. Pimp C's verse was coming on, just as we pulled into the parking lot of the packed Ray of Hope International Church.

I know, 'Big Pimpin' is an odd song to pull into a church parking lot bumping. Oh well, some preachers were Big Pimpin! But not Minister Brown. He put it down like Brandy and Chris Brown!

Ashley parked and got my crutches out of the back seat. I was ready for some good, anointed gospel! God, I needed a Spiritual Healing. I prayed to God, "Lord, help me get through this."

Ashley opened the door and gave me my crutches. She helped me out of the car, and then grabbed my baby out of the car seat.

"Awwe. She so sweet. Little Cry Cry. Cry Cry, wipe your eye eye." Ashley joked.

I struggled to get up, and balanced myself on the crutches.

"Biiiietch! Come get it!"

"Hold . . ." I fell. One girl kicked me. Two other girls stomped me.

Deonna snatched the crutches out of my hand. I couldn't do anything! Karate was no good with one leg!

Deonna beat me; hard. All I could do was cover my head.

Vanilla Bean, Shawty Rock, and Kim kicked me. I knew the three strippers were Joe's people! Kim was some red chick that he used to poke from the county—Montezuma, or whatever. Deonna, was beating me like I broke into her mama's house. I knew why they were doing it. It had to be because of Joe; jealous, I guess.

"Don't move, chick. Nothing personal," Chris Tye Rock said, aiming the gun at my baby and Ashley!

"Nooo! Don't shoot my baby!" my adrenaline rushed.

I rose up, pushing all the girls out the way and charged for the Bankhead nigga that had that gun.

Pow!

He fired.

I still tackled him, knocking the gun out of his hand.

Ashley held Crymeka close, and picked up the gun with her right hand.

"Yall hoes don't move," she said, with the gun in her right, and my baby in her left.

I was bleeding like a lady on her period, and trapped in a razor wire at the same time! But the love of a mother for her child was too strong. I would die for my baby! Take bullets for her! My life was not going good in any way, but I'd be damned if anybody would aim a gun at my baby! I came out of that ass whopping like the matrix man, when three-hundred people were beating him. I was lying on top of him, head all cracked up. My pretty face was bruised. I was lying on top of him, my leg in pain, and blood dripping on him.

"Look lil mama, put that gun down. Her baby daddy paid us a thousand a piece to beat her up anywhere we saw her, and to make her bleed. I got a baby, and I need the money. It's hard out here for a pimp! You wanna shoot somebody, shoot him," Deonna said, and walked off.

I just cried.

"Miss, I'm pushing you off me now. Talk to Joe. I needed that thousand, sorry," Chris said.

"Damn, that's messed up," Ashley said, stunned.

"What's wrong with Erica?" Reverend Brown said.

I just looked up at my preaching cousin, Joshua and cried. He and Ashley helped me into the church.

Deacon Fab was praying for me until the ambulance came.

"Honey, I been through so much with men; beating on me, cheating on me. Baby, I stayed single for twenty years. No sex. I will do bad by myself. I ain't letting anybody dog me out. I'm a woman. I would rather wait on the man that God sends me, than to be lied to, beat on, hurt, and dogged out. Put it in God's hands. That's the only one that won't let you down. When you put your trust in humans, they will fail you. Best friends, boyfriends, kids, and family. I love you, Erica. Give it to God," Evangelist Hannah Sheppard told me.

I cried. She held me. I loved her. She was so holy and righteous. I needed that glow, from God. This man, Joe, had the nerve to send girls to a church to beat me up, in front of my baby, and paid them five-thousand dollars when he ain't even spent fifteen dollars on pampers! Plus, he sent someone with a gun! On my baby! His baby! This man was a beast-arrogant and dirty!

They sat with me until the ambulance came again to take me back to the hospital.

"What the he . . . , I mean, heaven is going on with you?!"

Oh Lord, guess who walked in? My twinny twin twin, Keysha, was in the church popping bubble gum, like a ghetto couchie star! Her skirt was short enough to strike a match if she were to fart! And then, it was leather with a damn cross on both butt cheeks! Keysha was too damn much! In her all red leather! Skin tight! You could see my sister's nipples! They were as large as a quarter!

"Guuurl, what keep going on with you? I mean . . . (loud bubble gum smacking pause . . .) I mean, what's up with this nigga shooting at my twin? This is enough."

"Let God handle it." The one and only Bushwick, AKA Chocolate Thunder, said.

Chocolate Thunder was a choir director that could sing like Kelly, but he was a male stripper at night! Simpson Rd. Hard head.

"The Lord can handle it, after we handle it! This is my sister, no matter how much we fight, blood is thicker than water. Blood in, blood out! Excuse me Tim Jackson, and Rev. Joshua, but this nigga got to pay! Today!" Keysha PissedOff Brown yelled madder than the Tasmanian Devil!

Oh yea, believe it or not, me and my twin did kick some serious butts! I remember when this five-foot tall girl named Big Bird, who repeated kindergarten five times, walked up to me and snap! She walked right up and snatched my brand new number two pencil out of my hand, and broke it in half!

"Oooooh!" the entire class said. Everybody and the principal was scared of Big Bird!

Whack!

"Nobody messes wit my twin sister!" Keysha said. She stood on top of her desk, and dove off of it, like a wrestler jumping off the top rope!

She whacked Big Bird on top of her head with a five inch thick Webster dictionary! Keysha knocked her out with that dictionary!. Big Bird made straight A's, went to college, and later became an English professor! Ha, ha.

"Erica, the paramedics are here," Minister Chocolate Thunder informed me.

Chocolate Thunder was so ugly in the funniest, cutest way! He looked like Flava Flav, mixed with a cute, black, French poodle. He had the swag of Wesley Snipes! I loved Bushwick! He could sang! He sang to me all the way to the ambulance!

Talking 'bout, "This little light of mine, I'm gonna let it shine. Let it shine, let it shine, let it shine."

Hand clap . . .

The two paramedics gave Minister Bushwick, AKA Chocolate Thunder, Jackson a standing ovation. Then, they lifted me into the ambulance. I was so tired of the damn hospital. Damn. Evangelist Sheppard was right. I need Jesus, but heck, I even got beat up at church!

MOB UP!

"Dogs, mount up! Blatt! Blood and Mob, meet me at the Red House on Simpson Rd!" Keysha said.

Zoom! Zoom! Zoom! Zoom!

Santana, Trapp, Usef, Yae, Bubble Gum, Summer Hill, Skooter, Puncho, N.O. (New Orleans), O.G. Hood, Dog Man, JB, Chi, D.J., Scott, Black, Seaport, Sharlay, Champ, Meachie, and even Chocolate Thunder raced to the house to mob up, when Keysha made her Mob call.

Keysha left the door wide open. She was sitting with her legs wide open, smoking on Keysha, sitting with a red boned dike named Keysha, and listening to Keysha on the stereo!

Everyone came in, one by one. Keysha wondered why everyone who walked in, gave her an off guard, stank look. She didn't have on any panties, and boy did Keysha have a fat rabbit! A fat, curly haired rabbit at that!

"Keysha!"

"Yea, Uncle Hood?"

"Close your juice box," O.G. said, shaking his head.

"Oh. Ha, ha. Yea, this cat too fat. Listen yall, I know Joe is a Blood with rank, but enough is enough. I know his dad is connected, but he is in major violation. Erica was born a Blood, and Mob, and Gangsta at the same dang time, Mom is a Blood; dad a Gangsta from Zone 1. Now look, she is our family. He is our family . . ."

"Kill him," Trapp said.

"Naw, make him suffer!" San said.

"Yeah, cut his eyeballs out, so he can't see how to cheat," Kenya said, walking in the door, surprising everybody. They all stared, but quickly stop looking. This chick had a hand grenade in her hand!

"Look man, we need to just straight tell him that if he touch her again, he dies," uncle Chi said.

"Naw, kill him." That's all Trapp knew. You violate Trapp, death was your only punishment. The high rank Nine Trey gangsta was on his killa shit! Straight up!

"Man, let's fuck that nigga up!" O.G. Hood yelled.

"Let me get him," Kenya said.

Quietness. Everyone paused, and then looked at Kenya's stomach. She lifted her shirt up.

"He raped me."

Everyone took deep swallows.

Keysha started coughing. Her girlfriend Booch had to pat her on her back. Keysha's toughness disappeared. She had flashbacks of Joe raping her.

"Yea. He drugged me. I don't know what the hell he put in my drink, but I thought he was Pimp City!" Kenya yelled in anger.

"It was the Boop Pill," Bubble Gum said.

"What?" O.G. Hood asked, confused.

"It's a new hallucinogenic, sex pill from Russia. If you drop it in a drink, in five seconds, you will totally forget who you are and get freakier than a prostitute on her birthday!" Bubble Gum explained.

"So, once you take it, Joe could say, "Hey, you my wife," and she would believe it," she explained.

"Kill him! Fuck that!" Uncle Chi said, now losing his always calm demeanor.

Santana whispered in his girl's ear, "Marissa, Ima kill that nigga myself. Ima get him."

"No, San. Don't kill him. God will handle it," Marissa said.

"Well, if I don't kill him, he will feel dead," San said looking extremely mean.

Santana was so angry and hot, that you could fry and egg on his forehead!

Like Nelly said, Its Getting Hot in Here!

Joe was on top of the world, with a Lil Weezy attitude. He didn't give a damn, and he didn't have a care in the world.

Joe was chilling in his eight bedroom mansion in Lithonia, GA. He decided to step out on his porch, in his red Polo boxers, Polo tank top, and Polo shower shoes, with the gold soles. All red on red. He had seven fine naked red bones lying on his red, leather smooth floor, and seven chocolate super fine girls in the other room.

He was standing on the porch, smoking a blunt of Keysha, when he saw a stupid, fine girl, with extremely long and wavy hair. She appeared to be Asian or Indian and black.

"Hey," Joe called.

She turned around, and looked at him. She was visiting the house across the street. She looked at him, and had to look twice. He was brand new fine! She had to rub her eyes. Was this Chris Breezy? Nelly? L.L.?

His body was ripped, and tatted up. He had the prison tats, swagg, and was super proud.

"What's your name?"

"Ash-Ashley," she answered, feeling shy. Ashley was so mad at herself! She was beautiful! Tyra Banks, American Top Model beautiful! She had never met a man that could make her stutter! This man was hot; like chocolate coming out of the oven!

"Come with me," Joe said, grabbing her hands, and leading her into his mansion.

"Hoes, disappear!" he demanded. All fourteen of his naked, fine girls instantly flew downstairs.

Ashley wanted to resist, but his cologne was smelling so good, his eyes were so charming, his swag was so turned up, and he had a big one! He was powerful. Every woman likes a man with power. A man that knew he was a boss; knew he was in charge.

"You drink?" he asked.

"No, no," she coughed.

"What's wrong, cutie?" he asked.

"Oh, no, nothing," she smiled like a three year old on a pink Big wheel.

"You drink?"

"No sir."

"Awwe, ain't that sweet. A good girl," Joe said, rubbing on Ashley's smooth, silky legs, getting close to the end of her skirt.

He stopped, then got face to face with her. She could smell the fresh gum on his breath, and he smelled the Heat by Beyoncé that she had on. Their eyes locked. She was mesmerized and hypnotized. She couldn't resist him. Then suddenly, quickly, he snatched away from her, leaving her eyes closed and lips poking out in the form of a kiss.

Joe stood up, and stared down at the five foot seven, one-hundred and ten pound, petite, fine, caramel, model figure.

"I'm getting so hot. Do you want anything at all to drink?"

She cleared her throat.

"Yea, water," she said as she stared at the eleven inches bulging out of his boxers.

Then she watched him walk away. She was staring at the sexy, cool, powerful swagger walk that he had. His tight calves had a 9mm tatted on each of them. She looked at the Atlanta Falcon, flying over the Georgia Dome tatted on his back.

Wake up Ashley! She thought. Never, ever having had a one night stand, and surely not a thirty minute stand. Forget the stick. She wanted the dick!

Joe came back, and handed her the water in a fourteen carat gold Atlanta Hawks glass. He got back to his new project. He started rubbing up her legs slowly, and kissing her neck passionately. He was breathing his breath of sex on her skin, squeezing her butt, and sending chills through her body.

Click. He turned on the delicate love making sounds of Miguel. He laid her on her back on the couch. They began to wrestle with hunger and thirst. One was rock vein hard; the other was slip and slide wet.

"Stop!" Ashley screamed.

"What?" Joe said with a fake innocent glare.

"I can't do this. I don't know you."

"You didn't know your own mom until you got used to her. You are born not knowing anyone. But it's cool," he said, and handed her the water.

Quickly, she grabbed the golden glass, and fanned the hot, sex heat off of her. She turned the glass up to her lip. Joe pretended to watch ESPN. He anxiously watched her drink out of the side of his eyes.

Nope!

Something was wrong. Ashley allowed the glass to touch her lip, then she looked into the glass.

"A pill!" she yelled.

Wack!

He smacked it out of her hands. He turned from Lover boy to woman beater in two seconds! He threw her on the couch.

"Ouch!"

She kicked him in his nuts, and ran for the front door.

He bent over in pain.

Bang!

He threw a 8 ball at her.

"Dang!" she screamed, when the eight ball hit her left thigh, causing the slim cutie to hit the floor.

Ashley had no idea this was Erica's man. He walked up on her with a knife. Her pretty eyes filled with fear.

Pow. Pow. Boom. Boom. Boom. Boom.

Rapid, ricocheted bullets sprayed and splattered through the house, knocking out and shattering eighteen windows.

Keysha, Big Baby, Chocolate Thunder, Mad Marissa, Gator, Dog Man, Champ, Chi, O.G., Bubble Gum, Roscoe, Porsche, Summerhill, Seaport, JB, Green, Black, G-shots, Bad Betty, Fab, Santana, Trapp, Usef, Yae, Skooter, Puncho, N.O., Black, D.J., Scott, Sharlay, Meachie, and Kenya all had Joe's house completely surrounded.

Joe crawled to the window, and saw twenty vehicles surrounding his mansion.

Yea. They came to kill! They wanted war!

"Dammit, war yall will get," Joe said. Then he ran to the kitchen while bullets shot past his body, like small dodge balls!

He dived to the sink, not grabbing a street sweeper, but grabbing HIS street sweeper!

Terminator style!

"Hoes, mount up!"

Immediately, fourteen naked, fine, sexy strippers appeared with AK 47's! The seven red bones ran out of the back door shooting. The seven chocolate girls ran out the front door shooting. Joe walked into his elevator in his chimney/fireplace and rode the silver elevator up to the roof of his house.

Boom! Boom! Boom! Bang! Bang! Bang! Bam! Zip! Zip! Kah Boom! Boo yah! Pow! Pow! Pow! Boom!

Mad gunfire. Intense war. Fire, bullets, smoke, flames, blood, bodies falling in all directions.

Boo yah! Boo yah!

Kenya PimpCity Brown threw two hand grenades and blew off the front door!

"Ha, ha! Look at yall! Look at yall, pitiful punks! My hoes shot better than yall! My strippers got more heart than yall! Blatt! Blatt! Blatt! Yall can't kill me! Yall mother fuckers can't kill Joe! I'm the brown-skinned Godzilla, mother fuckers! Boom! Boom!" Joe yelled.

He exploded a miniature pipe bomb, causing the green Escalade to explode! Now the car was on fire! Roscoe was down. The two chocolate, big booty strippers had shot him. Everyone outside had been shot at least twice except Kenya and Joe, the hoe! Joe couldn't be touched! He was protected like the first black President! He was completely surrounded by a bulletproof glass on the top of his roof, and he was firing his weapon through a hole just big enough for the barrel to fit through.

Umph!

"Nigga, you forgot about me," Ashley said, throwing a knife directly into the back of his neck, at the top of his spine.

Joe's eyes got big as a porn star's booty hole! He dropped down on one knee.

"Damn."

He nearly pissed himself. He turned around, and saw Keysha, who was shot and bleeding out of her left arm. Kenya, with a pink AK. Ashley, with a hammer and a butcher knife, and yeah . . . me, Erica with a bazooka!! His worst nightmare! All the females that he either fucked, raped, or tried to rape. It all backfired!

"Time to meet your Maker," I said with not one bit of regret or remorse in my eyes. I was filled to the top, like an over packed pot of hot, popping grits.

All four of us aimed our weapons. Ashley prepared to throw her knife. She used to shoot squirrels from a long distance in Griffin with guns. She had the best aim in Griffin, GA, and maybe the world.

I was the most hurt girl in the world. I finally had Joe at my mercy. His gun was down in front of him, and he was now on both knees.

He didn't show any emotion. He didn't give a damn one way or the other.

"Yall hoes get it over with," Joe said.

So, we got it over with!

"Noooooooooooo! Don't !" a voice yelled.

We all turned around simultaneously.

"Don't kill my brother!" Daja yelled, dressed in all white Versace, with Timberland boots, and a white hat. She had cute, all red braids in her hair.

I stared at Daja and then at Joe with tears and anger in my eyes. Everyone was quiet. Even the air stood still. Time stopped. No one spoke for one, two, three, four, five, six, seven, eight, nine, ten seconds...

"I got him," the foxy, female detective, McDowell said.

"Me and Miss Walker already know. We'll just clean this World War Four Hood Battle up," the brown, sexy and short, but powerful female detective said.

The cops, detectives, and ambulances crowded the streets like a Beyoncé concert! Rachel from Channel 5 News was live. The helicopter hovered over the house as the FBI and SWAT team arrived.

"We finally got him," FBI agent, Jackson said.

"Yeah, we been waiting to get Joe Brown for three years! We got him!" Detective Jamison said.

Zoom. Zoom.

Trapp and Santana raced out of the scene, zooming past police cars. Both were shot in the leg. Vanilla Bean and Deanna were two of the fine girls who hopped on their motorcycles and got away. Dog Man, AKA Owens, complained, "Damn! They got me for life this time!"

Holding his wounded knee, he knew he was going straight back to prison for life! Dog Man! Damn, he forgot he had a pocket full of heroin too!

DOWN FOR THE COUNT

Finally, Joe was down, like a casket in the grave. The knife was in the back of his neck. Blood was oozing from the young thug's neck.

"Stop the bleeding! Apply pressure!" the pretty, thick nurse Leslie yelled.

They tried every trick in the life saving book. Nothing worked. Blood continued to pour!

"Maybe it hit an artery!"

"Maybe he's paralyzed."

I stood there and watched, hoping he would die. Daja ran toward her brother and got down on her knees, crying.

"Noooooo! Bro, don't die on me!" she cried. Joe was more than her brother. He was like her twin brother. They were closer than Keysha and I ever were.

"Get her away, before we lose him!" Nurse Mickens ordered.

"Please stay away," Chief FBI Detective McDowell yelled, grabbing the wild and shocked, Daja.

Daja started yelling and yanking the braids out of her hair!

I just watched . . . . hoping he would die. I couldn't feel any pain. No hurt, sadness, fear, or remorse. Why should I? He took me through years of embarrassment, hurt, shame, miscarriage, beatings, cheating, disrespect, jail, and unhealed drama.

I balled up my fists, and waited on him to die. Daja was crying, and acting Mental Health Level Four!

So what? Your brother was a terrible person that deserved to die! I even cracked a sneaky smile. They couldn't save the dirty bastard. Kenya, Ashley, and Porsche just stared, while the paramedics hooked up the IV.

Over!

Like Jason on Friday the 13th part one-hundred! Joe rose to his feet, snatching the knife out the back of his tatted up neck.

"Yall hoes waitin' on Joe to die?! It won't happen! Yall hoes waitin' on Joe to cry?! It won't happen! Joe Brown won't die! Real Niggas don't die!" Joe yelled like an insane inmate, who constantly cut his own body for attention.

"Mr. Brown, please calm down. It's over," Detective McDowell said.

Joe stared down at the brown, short, super sexy detective, and kissed her.

"It ain't over!" he demanded.

Boom!

Then Joe collapsed.

I LOVE AND HATE YOU

"Yeah, I love you, and I hate you at the same dang time," I told Joe, as he lay up in the hospital bed, motionless.

"Paralyzed?" I asked R.N. Bailey.

"Yes, sweetie. Mr. Brown is paralyzed from his neck, down. He may get his feeling back; he may not," she informed me.

Loud, deafening crying . . .

I held my baby, as she cried. It felt good, looking at Joe Brown, motionless. It felt good, but it also hurt. However, there would be no more pain, no more drama, no more fights. Hours went by, then weeks, then months. Nothing. No movement.

"Damn! When is my brother waking up?" Daja asked, holding her fiancé's hand.

"I know. It's hard looking at him like this," I admitted.

I sat by his side every day and night, rubbing his hand, kissing his face. Ringtone . . . Nikki Minaj and Drake's song. I looked at my red iPhone and laughed.

"What it do, Shawty?" I asked.

"I need to holla at you," Keysha said.

I kissed Joe, hugged Daja, and peeled off in the Maybach. My heart was so heavy. I was listening to Yolanda Adams. Only gospel music could heal my heart.

"Damn!"

I almost crashed when I saw it! I was pregnant, again!

THE JOKE'S ON YOU

"I love you bro, forever. I'm always here for you. No matter what." Daja told her brother, as she rubbed his hands and cried. She hated that not only was he paralyzed, but he was also so heavily sedated with drugs, that all he could do was sleep.

"Let's pray for bro," Champ said. He started, "Dear, Lord, in the name of Jesus, King of Kings, sweet Jesus. Heal our brother. By your stripes, we are healed."

"Amen. Amen. Amen." Daja cried.

"In the mighty name of Jesus, we pray. Amen." Champ prayed.

"God, I can't believe it. Twelve months, and not a word from him!"

"He will heal. Have faith, Daja."

She kissed her brother, and left the room.

"Dammit man!" Joe said, when they left. He peeped out of his eyes, and watched everyone leave.

"I love this fake dead crap," he said. Then he looked at his five hundred thousand dollar platinum Rolex. Midnight!

"Time to growl and I ain't talkin bout ware wolves!" he joked. He pushed his button. The door to his room opened very slowly, like someone was sneaking in to kill him.

Someone wanted revenge. Little did they know, Joe had a .44. Finally, the person was in his room. Joe had his gun aimed at the door.

"Put that thang down," the nurse said.

"Oh, hey sweet cat," he laughed, and pulled her onto his lap.

Nurse Harris sat on his lap, and touched his soft lips with her index finger.

"Quiet, you tiger," she said, smiling as she grinded on his wood.

"I thought you wasn't coming tonight?" he said, hard as a brick wall in China.

"Naughty, naughty boy. D. Harris always coming at midnight. Haven't I come every night for twelve months straight?"

"Yea. Except your damn days off."

"Ha, ha. Lay down." Nurse Harris pushed him on the bed. "Uncage my monster. Let me do my favorite! Ride. Ride. Ride! In my Ciara voice."

They both wrestled to get it out, while she lay on top of him, and kissed him like a thirsty, faithful girlfriend, who had been waiting faithfully two years for her man to get out of prison.

They kissed, and kissed.

"Awww, daddy," she said when he slid inside her wetness.

She grabbed his neck, chest, and face, and rode while her eyes rolled to the back of her head.

"Up! Get up!" he yelled in anger.

She ignored him, continued to ride, and jiggled each cheek, making him weak, and hot like a freak.

Joe regained his strength, and picked her up. Boom!

He flipped her over. He stood bare feet on the popsicle cold hospital floor, and beat her from the back, as she raised her juicy behind in the air, on the bed.

He stood up, and pounded her. They sweated for exactly thirty strong minutes.

"Ok. Lunch break over!" she said, laughing and pulling away.

"Hey, what are yall doing?!" a female yelled, causing both of them to turn their heads like owls.

"Like, who the hell are you?" Nurse Harris said, looking like a short, chocolate, tasty, Swiss roll. She was four foot nine, one hundred and nine pounds.

"Naw, the question is, what the hell was yall doing?" Nurse Bean asked.

They looked at each other, scratching their heads.

"I want answers!!!" Nurse Bean yelled. She then jumped on top of Joe, and kissed him!

They all laughed when Vanilla took off her old grey, curly, old lady wig, any laid it on the table.

"Gotcha!" Vanilla laughed.

"Biiietch! Ima kill you!" Deonna said, holding her chest.

"I know right?! Ha, ha, girl. Yall better be more careful," Vanilla joked, looking like a spectacular, young Lauren London.

The two young nurses were best friends, and Joe's two main jack girls!

Jack girls are robbers. They were both as fine as strippers. One chocolate; one caramel. They both made men melt, then hit them with bullet proof belts!

Whap!

They would rob a nigga quick!

"How much you make tonight?" he asked the gangsta cuties.

"Shiiit. I just milked Dr. Wize, and made that skinny, burnt face, mule mouth, fish tank breath, fart sniffing, cross eyed, intelligent, dumb ass out of fifty thousand dollars!" Vanilla bragged, flipping through her hundreds.

"Ha, ha. You little slut. How you get Dr. DoDo?" Deonna asked.

"Girl, I talked to him. I recorded his needle penis ass on my phone begging for sex. I told him I was gonna play it on the intercom for the entire hospital to hear!"

They all laughed.

"Awe, hell. I feel bad," Dee said, holding her head down.

"Why?" Joe asked.

"Cause, nigga! I only made a hundred racks!" Deonna bragged.

"Whaaat?! A hundred racks on racks," Joe laughed, walking around the room rubbing his chinny chin chin.

"Get back, slut. Watcha do?" Vanilla asked, bumping her arm. Hand on her waist, wanting to know how her down south girl topped her.

"Now see. That's the shit I don't like! Ha, ha. I met a rapper at Pimp City Strip Club. His name is the opposite of Future. His name was Past . . ." she paused.

Joe froze, hand on chin. They all laughed, so Deonna continued.

"Anyways, gurl, we sat in his car. He had a black and gold Jaguar. So he asked me if I smoke loud. I said yeah. He said he was from New Orleans. I said oh, take me to Pimp City. He had no idea where that was, so we parked on Glenwood and Candler Rd, got some gas, and Earl and Philly shot his ass! Fat Daddy took his car, with me in it. They drove to Jalisa's house, behind Krystal's restaurant, to strip the car down, at the chop shop. While they were all talking, I decided to pop the trunk, and booyah! One-hundred brand new thousand dollars, slut! In a money, money, money bag! I got a ride from Noel, and went straight to the house," Deonna said, cheering. She gave Vanilla a high five.

"Wat up?" Joe said, waving for them to calm down, while he answered his phone.

"I got the whole thang."

"One hundred boops?" Joe asked.

"Yea. One hundred boops. I'm on the third floor, by the snack machine."

"Bet that. I'll be down there," he told Noel.

Boops was the code word for anything illegal! Mr. Pimp City created the Boop when he was in Augusta prison. One hundred Boops meant one hundred thousand.

Joe and the nurses left the room. He got off the elevator. Noel had his back turned, trying to decide what snack button to push, for the Skittles.

"Boo!"

"What the . . ."

Pow! Gunshot! Glass shattering.

The bullets sprayed the snack machine, and the drink machine, hitting Noel once in his shoulder.

"Ahhh!" he held his shoulder, and hit the ground.

"Caught you, Joe!" I said, busting him out.

"Damn Erica, you a fool."

"Naw nigga, you a fool!" I said, all up in his face.

"What you mean?"

"I mean, you smell like sex, nigga!" I said, sniffing him, and looking him dead in his eyes.

I knew he was guilty. I knew the look.

"Ummm, what?"

"Joe, when were you gonna tell me your girls were nurses on third shift? You been fucking and sucking every night for twelve months straight, keeping it a secret, and pretending you were paralyzed, to cover your ass from the cops and robbers! I been selling your dope, maintaining your house, cars, and baby. Now I'm three months pregnant, again! And you up here fucking the nurses!"

You just don't know how mad this dirty dick nigga had me!

"Nigga, you make my nipples itch! I'm out!" I said, throwing the 9mm down, and walking away.

Bam! He punched me in the head.

"You do what I say! It's Joe's way, or no way!" Joe yelled, standing over me.

"Give me this shit!" he said, snatching my purse.

"All this belongs to me," he said, taking my money out of my purse.

"And what were you doing with Trapp and D.J. last night?!" he roared, picking up the gun, standing over me.

He was fire hot! Hotter than a forest fire in Africa, on the Fourth of July. His eyes were as red as a dragon's after smoking on Keysha!

"Tell me! I'll kill you, slut! Erica! I will kill you! I made you!" he yelled.

I was looking pitiful. Nothing I could say would make it better. No man wanted another man around his main woman. It was a man thang. A pride thang. I couldn't tell him they only came by to drop off his money. Who told him?

"Erica, do you think I'm playing with you?! I will kill you right here in this damn hospital, and get away with it!"

"Hey man, let that go . . ."

Pow!

"Let yo tongue out of me and my slut business, nigga!" Joe said, shooting the dude smack in the head, in front of the camera, with no care at all.

"I will blow your head completely off of your pretty, pregnant body, Erica Brown. Slut, I made you. Let me even get a hunch, that you fucked my friend, and Ima kill you!" Joe yelled.

I didn't like this side of Joe Brown. I was scared. He already shot me once, broke my nose, and arm. This nigga was crazy enough to end my book right now!

Pow! Pow!

"Noel, get this and go. I'm bout to kill this hoe!"

Noel looked at Joe, picked up the dope, and left the money, money bag. Stozzi, the sexy Decatur singer/rapper was waiting on him at the door. She was wearing some boy shorts that made her look so fine, you could slap your mama. Well, maybe your great grandma!

Slice . . .

Stozzi sliced his throat.

"Damn," he said.

His eyes were bigger than the death of Abraham Lincoln. He knew he was dead, by the hands of the fine, sexy, stupid thick, exotic singer, star, Stozzi.

Pow!

Joe finished him.

"Nigga taking too long to die. This ain't no damn drama movie! Slut, this Real Life Action!"

Joe grabbed my hair, and drug me out the door, after he shot the security guard in the head for trying to snatch Noel's drugs.

WAM!

With his right leg, Joe kicked open the double door, an inch away from Stozzi's hips. He drug me with his left hand, by my long, wavy hair. He held the money in his right hand. I had blood rushing through my eyes. My head was in excruciating pain. I felt like I had a migraine headache delivered by Satan himself. Damn! There goes my new hairdo. I could feel him pulling my hair out of my scalp. He tossed me down in front of the elevator, like trash. Then, he picked me up, threw me over his shoulder, and carried me to the Maybach.

"Damn Joe, why you do that girl like that?" Stozzi asked.

Uh. Oh. Why did she have to say that? Like Jason, Joe quickly turned around and shot her.

Boom!

Stozzi was gone like the year 2000.

Joe focused his attention back to me. "Biiitch, be still!" he said, and slammed the door.

This fool had on no drawers, only an open, blue and white hospital gown, standing on the curve. However, it was one o'clock in the morning, and not a soul was visible.

I just cried, and held my stomach as this fool drove me down I-75 south to the damn middle of nowhere! Where was he taking me? Did he plan on killing me, and dumping my body in the woods? Knowing him, maybe he would just pistol whip me, and make me suffer.

Bam!

"Oh, God!" I held my chest from the devastating, hard, impacting blow. A deer had ran in front of the Maybach!

"Dammit! Another half a million dollars down the drain! Slut, you bad luck! It's your fault! You got the devil in your damn pussy! God tryna tell me something. You a hoe! You fuckin my homeboys! Slut, I ain't never seen a deer in my damn life! Now all of a sudden, I hit one! Nobody on the planet crashes two damn Maybachs! Time your black, pregnant, suicide pussy ass get in the car, the mother fucker crashes! Slut, you sellin two hundred thousand dollars worth of pussy! You payin' for my shit! Get out, slut! Walk. Hitch hike! Show your legs! Slut, don't hold your stomach! Fuck that baby! Yea, you fucked me in the hospital for twelve months, but slut, that's Trapp's baby! Or, maybe it's San's baby. Yall hoes know yall fuck yall cousins. What the fuck you bitchin' and whining for?"

Smack!

"Ouch!"

He back slapped me instantly, busting my pretty top lip, and messed up my lip gloss! He still looked furious!

Scrrrreeeech!

The car slid, front tire rolled off, and the brakes yelled! He stopped in the middle of the damn expressway!

Boom.

A truck smashed a small black Benz.

Joe quickly turned the car off the expressway, to the side of the dark woods. He got out the car. I wanted to turn and run or wave for help, but it was worthless. It was pitch black outside.

He walked to the front of the car, shook his head; hand rubbing that damn chin. I just cried. I curled up in the front seat, thinking about my daughter. What was she doing? CryMeka was with my mom, and I know my niece, Bre'Shauna, was probably trying to teach her how to sing.

"Ahhh!" I whined when he punched me on top of my head. Now, I had the biggest migraine headache ever known to mankind. I wish I could pay Trapp and them to kill this nigga. Tie him up to a spaceship, and drop his ass off on the moon! And Boop!

"Get out."

Thump. Thump.

He snatched me out of the car, and drug me into a house. It was rocky, and dirty as hell. My head was bleeding. He picked me up, dropped me on the floor, then kissed me!

"I'm sorry! I love you!" Joe Brown, the devil's son, told me.

I looked up at him like a stranger. He raped me; forced himself inside me. It didn't feel the same. I couldn't get turned on from the excruciating pain, hurt, anger, and fear. I just lay there motionless for minutes while he stroked. I had tears longer than the Mississippi River rolling down my face.

Where was I?

After he came, he picked me up, and tied me to a damn small, steel, twin sized, Georgia prison bed. He wrapped a chain around both of my legs and waist.

"I will feed you. But I can't let you fuck while you pregnant with my baby. I'll kill all them niggas. Joe Brown can't die. I love you. Pookie will take care of you. If you need something, call her. I'm gone," he said, then left.

That's it? Like, when was he coming back? Who in the hell is Pookie? A pit bull? A hyena? A seven foot tall muscle man?

"Hey, I'm Pookie," a voice said. I know I was beautiful, but I felt bruised and ugly. My long, wavy hair was messy. My body was cut up and bleeding.

"You're pretty. He told me to watch you."

"Where am I?"

"Can't tell you."

"You look young. How old are you, girl?" I asked the yellow, short haired, tatted up, baby doll.

Was this nigga crazy? Lord, was Joe a child molester too?

"I'm seventeen. I'm legal."

"Why are you here? Where are you from? Where are your parents? Did Joe touch you?"

She looked away from me, and walked off with her head down.

RIDING ROUND, GETTIN' IT!

Joe left the small house on the dirt road, off of Gordon Highway in Augusta. He was flying up I-20 West like the first black race car driver that actually won a race!

Joe was blastin' the ATL rapper, 2 Chains. "All I want for my birthday is a big booty girl! . . . You in First Place"

Today was his birthday, and he was about to throw down, Joe Brown style! I was not allowed! He pulled the fat blunt of Keysha, sipped on some Erica, called up Lisa, and got some head from Tamicya!

"Damn, it feels good to be Joe Brown," he said smiling, while patting Tamicya on her head like a cute pound puppy!

"I know, daddy," she said, humming on him, and staring into his powerful eyes, with her big, beautiful, seducing, innocent, pretty eyes. She was only sixteen, however, already the best Joe Brown has had!

Joe curled his legs, and sped! He could give a Georgia, jailhouse, shower shoe hell, about his pregnant baby mama, Erica!

Pookie was actually sixteen, pretending to be seventeen. Just like Tamicya was sixteen, pretending to be twenty-one! Dammit it, Pookie could watch her! The yellow, adorable, young, tatted up cutie was very obedient. Joe had kidnapped the kid from her parents, and gave her one thousand dollars a week, and a 2014 yellow Benz, just to look after everyone he took to his hidden house in Augusta, GA.

Plus, she could cook like a down south, slap your mama, grandma! Pookie had more tats than Weezy Weeze! Erica would be just fine! He smiled, and enjoyed his moment with the hottest, freakiest, young porn star in America.

Luda came on the mix C.D.

'You represent for the women all across the world . . . Sit on the front row, and watch me perform . . .'

Joe cruised to the hotel in Riverdale, and parked.

He got out, and two fine, China doll-looking, yellow bones opened the door. They were already birthday suit naked.

"Hey, daddy."

"Oooo wee! Who is this young tender you brought for us daddy"

"Ha, ha. Yall hoes behave," Joe said.

Bam! Bam!

Tamicya went off! She punched both of the twin dolls in the temple, knocking them clean out, like dirty clothes!

Joe spinned, and looked at her.

"Dam, I didn't know you was a mean slut."

Bam!

She punched him.

Pow!

He shot her in the head.

"Oh well. Now you are a dead slut. West side, clean this hoe up," he told his short, west Atlanta homeboy, who was laying on the bed, with two more fine, chocolate, super thick girls.

West-side had a kilo of cocaine, and twenty pounds of Keysha on the bed.

"Bet that down, cause she just got Booped!" West-side said, laughing.

Joe looked at his homeboy, with that evil, Joe Brown, killa nigga eye.

"Don't make me Boop! yo ass," Joe said, staring at West-side with his green glock 40.

West-side stared up at him.

Bloop!

He dropped the dead body that he had picked up.

"Ha, ha, nigga, get somewhere. This room been jumping and the hoes been humping! It's three hundred thousand under the mattress. That's what we made today. Happy B-day, nigga!" West-side said, giving Joe a bloody hug!

"Ah, yeah. Ha, ha. That's what's up, my nigga. Erase this dead dumb ass. I got ten more stops to make. Good looking, Dog," Joe said, collecting the cash.

YOU GOT IT BAD

Throw back Usher, 'You Got it Bad,' beat like a down south house party, in the small hidden house.

"The food smell good Pookie, but I'm pregnant. Can you please untie me?" I asked the young girl, holding my stomach.

She didn't even look at me.

"Eat this," she said, and walked away.

"How?" I asked, feeling too weak to fuss or fight. I had been in the house for two days, with no food. Only water, and what seemed to be sleeping pills.

"Heeeey! Trick off Tuesday! Get up!" Joe yelled, coming into the house with Vanilla and Tameka.

They both had on tiny pink bathing suits.

"You ain't dead yet?" he asked, looking down on me.

I just stared up at the devil. I knew in my mind, it was over. I knew it. My FIRST love is my WORST love.

"You like porn?" he asked me, French kissing Tameka. Their tongues dangling out of each other's mouths, like two loving snakes.

"Well, that's great, cause me and the girls are about to do a foursome for you. Live. Live porn, baby! Wooh! Boop! Boop!!!" he laughed as he kissed the two giggling girls.

Yeah, if I ever get loose, Ima give their asses a foursome they can't remember! Four knocks to their skulls!

He had one girl in each arm, pulling their bottoms down, playing inside them with his fingers. Tameka got on her knees, and went to lick, suck, heaven! Then, she bent over while he tongue kissed Vanilla and spanked Tameka on her giggling booty.

She was red, with tats all over her big booty, and she had a slim waist, and pretty, green eyes. Too bad those green eyes would turn midnight black, once I got loose!

"Pookie! Get over here, and join in, you high yellow, young, whore!" Joe demanded.

Pookie was so cute and shy. She never uttered more than three words in two days.

Smack!

"Meka, yall go get on Pookie," Joe said, smacking Tameka on her booty, and making her go grab Pookie, as he eased out of her. Vanilla was still kissing him all over his chest and moaning.

Pookie was sitting down, about to cry, with her pretty, puppy doll, watery eyes.

The twenty-five year old stripper quickly hopped onto her lap, gave her a kiss, and a lap dance. She grinded her naked booty on Pookie's legs. Then, she went for another kiss on her forehead. Next, she put her nipples on Pookie's pretty lips.

Pookie had more water in her eyes than Miami Beach!

"Don't be shy little mama, kiss 'em."

Woosh! Bam! Bam! Smack! Crack! Whack! Kick! A-town Stomp!

From out of nowhere, the once innocent, harmless, Pookie punched the girl all the way across the room. Zoosh! Then, she did a two video game cart wheel flip across the room in two split seconds! She power punched the girl two times in the eye, then chopped her across the neck, then picked up a wooden chair, and broke it across her head. BANG!

Next, she slapped her, kicked her with her pink Polo boots, then jumped in the air, and A-town stomped the trick's head in the ground, instantly breaking her neck!

"I don't want to have sex!" Pookie yelled, with her small fists balled up, looking like a mean, young, yellow dragon.

Vanilla's eyes got bigger than a pregnant pig's booty.

"Oh well, another good piece of pussy gone down the drain," Joe shrugged.

"I'm a virgin, and will stay a virgin until I get married!" Pookie said, walking right up in Joe's face, then getting in Vanilla's face.

"Whatever," Joe said, then walked up to me.

"Hungry, honey?" he asked.

Twah.

I spit on him. He wiped his face, then laughed.

"Chow call!" he said.

Then Joe removed the chains off my waist, leaving my legs chained up, and unchained my arms.

I was too weak to raise up on the small jail built, iron bed.

"Thanks," I told Pookie, as she helped me up.

Pookie was instantly as calm as a library straight A-nerd. She fed me, holding the hot, creamy potatoes to my mouth. It was soooo good! I ate that junk with my eyes closed.

"Owww!"

"Too hot?" Pookie asked.

I shook my head, and she blew the spoon, then continued to feed me. Next, she chopped up the New York strip steak.

"Ummmm. So good." I said.

"Drink?" she asked me, like a shy kid.

I motioned my head, yeah.

She brought the gold cup of fruit punch to my mouth.

Bam!

Kool-Aid splashed all over my face.

"Gotcha!" Joe yelled, laughing, with his tongue sticking out, and pointing his finger at me.

I just looked at that fool.

"Boop!" the woody wood pecking idiot said.

"Daddy!"

"What the hell?" I said out loud, forgetting my pain and quickly rejuvenating.

I turned my head quicker than a McDonald's door on a downtown Friday evening.

"Who is that girl?" I asked Joe, stunned.

"That's my daughter," Pookie said, staring at Joe, with tears in her eyes.

"What?!"

Now I was double lost. Like, was I living in a story? A matrix? A sitcom? A book? This nigga, Joe Brown, was a book! Every page of his life was something new!

"That's Aaliyah, my first born. Remember that Christmas/family reunion, in our 12th grade year? At Columbia High? When I came two hours late for our Christmas Dinner in College Park? Your best friend, Kim, was having our baby. That's right. Beautiful little Aaliyah! Hey, don't she look like the mixed, yellow version of Aaliyah, the singer? Ha. Ha. Ima wild boy. Ima, Ima wild boy," Joe boasted, giving me all kinds of embarrassing betraying shock.

Kim was my best friend in high school. She was pregnant by Santana! Or so we thought . . .

"I know, I know what you thinkin'. We had the whole school thinking it was Santana baby. Ha. Ha. Santana was too busy on his mob shit, with YMF, and G.F. He was in jail when she started showing, so San couldn't defend his self. So me and Kim pretended San was the dad. Of course, that's why Santana girlfriend, and Danika, Daja, and September beat Kim red ass! Seattle, Washington style!"

"Joe Brown, I hate you," I said, as I sat up on that hard as steel, prison bed.

My booty felt like it was naked on a damn ironing board! Dam! How did prisoners sleep on their small ass, steel beds for twenty years?!

"Nigga, yall had the whole school fooled!" I said, shaking my head.

"Yea, I raised her though. Kim left Montezuma, left Atlanta, and ran to damn Decatur, Illinois!"

"And, I been the one raising her," Pookie said, explaining why she called this beautiful, long-haired girl her daughter.

Aaliyah was adorable. She was just standing there, listening to us with her pretty eyes bucked, and her mouth open.

"Now, Kim punk ass up there in Virginia with her white, crack head daddy, Bob!" Joe said, looking very upset.

I remember Bob was the richest lawyer in Atlanta. He killed Kim's mom, Elizabeth, and only did seven years in prison!

"Joe, why are you doing me like this?" I asked, feeling so disgusted with this dog, mutt nigga.

Joe Brown had to be the worst nigga, worst boyfriend, worst baby-daddy, worst every damn thing!

"Cause I can, dammit! Joe Brown do what the hell he wanna do, when he wanna do it. Anybody got a problem with it, they die. Now you shut the hell up, and sleep!"

Bam!

"Shiiiit!" I hollered, holding my instantly, closed up, black eye.

"Heelllp!" I yelled, as Joe tied me back to the steel bed, with the five inch thick chain around my waist and arms.

Pookie, Vanilla, and Aaliyah just started at me. I felt worse than a slave. I just hollered and cried, cried, cried, until I couldn't cry anymore. I cried until all the tears were out of my body. I tried kicking and yanking my arms, but to no prevail. I was stuck to die; sentenced to death, by Joe Brown!

Pregnant, kidnapped, hurt, and abused. I felt worthless; like a carton of white milk, in a high school food fight!

I seriously considered suicide! But why live in hell, then die, and go to hell?! SUICIDE is Double Hell! If I kill myself, that's the only sin I can't be forgiven for, because I'll already be dead, and can't pray!

Lord help me. Save me from the mighty wrath of Beat Down, Joe Brown!

Days passed by. Weeks passed by. Months passed by. Still chained to the bed. I didn't even see Joe again. Pookie started talking to me a little more. I would watch her and Aaliyah play.

Aaliyah was such a happy kid. She didn't realize the serious situation she was in.

"Aunty, Erica! When are you gonna get out of that bed, and quit playing dead?! Ha, ha", she laughed.

"Ah, girl. I told you, I'm just laying here until I have this baby, then Boop! I'm gone!" I replied, trying to smile, unable to squeeze out a laugh.

My belly was in too much pain. I was nine months pregnant. No check-ups, so I didn't have a clue what I was having.

The baby was kicking, hard, violent, and painful kicks, as if the baby was tired, and feeling mama's pain.

"Ouch! Ah! God, I'm hurting!"

"It will be ok, Aunty Erica. I'm rubbing the little baby," Aaliyah said, as she rubbed my big belly.

That actually calmed the baby down. So, I guess my baby liked Aaliyah. She was so beautiful and happy with her yellow skin, and long hair.

"Here, eat this, boo," Pookie said, offering me a bowl of hot vegetable soup.

Bam!

The bowl flew out of her hand.

"Ouch! Shiiit!" I yelled, 'cause the hot soup burned my chin.

Aaliyah was crying.

"Ahhhhh! Help me! Help me!" she cried.

Joe knocked the steaming hot soup out of Pookie's hand, and it flew all over Aaliyah's pretty face.

"Oh, baby, are you ok?!" Pookie said, running across the room to check her out for burns.

Aaliyah had her back against the wall, standing there scared to death, and shaking. Joe should not have hurt this kid.

"Ahh! My stomach! Dammit, Joe! This baby! Get over here, nigga!" I yelled in terrifying pain.

"Cool, I brought a nurse. Go deliver this slut baby," he told the nurse.

"I hate you, Joe! I hate you!"

"Calm down. Push, mam. Push."

The damn nurse looked like a stripper! This damn cross eyed whoremonger!

"Almost. I see the head. Come on. Co . . ."

"Shut up! Shut the hell up!"

"Push, push. It's out!" the nurse said, pulling my baby completely out of me.

Instantly, I forgot about all of my worries and pain. I forgot about my current kidnapping situation.

"Awww, let's weigh it," the nurse said, putting him on the scale.

"How much is my baby?" I asked.

"You got yourself a football player! Eight pounds, nine ounces."

Pookie unchained everything but my legs.

"His name is 3 Pac."

"What?!" I snapped.

"You heard me, 3 Pac," Joe repeated.

"So, let me get this straight. 3 Pac Brown?" the stupid nurse said, as she wrote the name down.

"Joe, you stupid. Bring me my baby," I said to the nurse.

She bent over to give me my little 3 Pac.

Bam!

"God!" the five foot tall, three hundred pound nurse cried.

The second Miss Biggy gave me my baby, I head-butted her smack between her eyes. Blood poured out of her nose like a water hose!

"What the?"

Bam!

Pookie hit Joe over the head with a five foot tall red lamp, before he could even finish his words.

"Untie me!" I told Pookie.

Joe was on the ground.

"Hold my baby, Pookie," I said.

"No! I'm kicking this nigga's ass too! He been mean to you, and he burnt Aaliyah!" Pookie yelled at me, with no understanding.

Pookie started kicking him.

Fuck it! I laid my crying baby on the bed, and went to work.

"You!"

Kick.

"Dirty!"

Kick.

"Low down!"

Kick.

"No good!"

Kick.

"Cheating!"

Kick.

"Lying!"

Kick.

"Evil!"

Kick.

"Woman beating!"

Kick.

"Dirty Dick!"

Kick.

"Son of a biiitch!"

Kick.

We were both kicking him. The kids were crying.

"Move," I pushed Pookie out of the way.

Bang!

I donkey kong, clobbered that nigga in the back of the head with the same thick chains he held me down with for all of these months.

He was unconscious, and blood was squirting out of his head, like he was a water hose. He went from looking like a pretty boy, to looking like a dead vampire on fire!

"I broke his face! I broke that nigga face!" I celebrated.

I tried to break every bone in that nigga face, with that chain! His nose, jaw, teeth, and all!

He was dead done. I didn't care. I almost felt better, but his penis was coming off as soon as I caught my breath.

Pookie stared in shock, scratched head, then sat down beside me on the bed. She hugged Aaliyah, while she stood up crying, barely audible, with snot running out her nose.

Her face was not visibly burnt from the hot soup.

Joe stood up . . .

We had our backs to Joe.

"Diiiiieeee!" he yelled.

We quickly turned around, shocked as a preacher at a 2 Chains concert!

Joe had his .45 in his hand. He stood up, looking like Jason vs. Godzilla!

Before Pookie, I, and the kids could react . . .

Pow!

Shots fired . . .

THE FAT LADY AND MAN SANG; OVER!

My baby! Aaliyah! Pookie! Me?

One of us was hit. He aimed directly towards us, fired and fell.

Joe Brown, never missed his target. I saw that nigga shoot a butterfly off of a building downtown, at Freak nick!

I checked my baby first, then Aaliyah, and looked Pookie up and down,

"It's over with . . ." Kenya PimpCity Brown said standing in the doorway with a red .44 Mangum in her hand. Double to my surprise, Daja stood beside her.

"It had to end, Erica." Daja said, tears in her eyes.

"Yeah, I wasn't gonna let you think that I fucked that dog ass nigga on purpose. So, what betta way to prove I was drugged and raped beside a silver bullet in the head! Vampire style! Woosh!" Kenya yelled.

"Oh, bring the dope, so we can make it look drug related," Daja told San, D.J., Hood, Trapp, and the six-foot, black and Chinese homie, big J.B.

They each poured two open bags of cocaine all over the house. Then the Gangsta Blood Mob crew all drove off. I grabbed my baby, and walked out the door. Pookie, and Aaliyah hopped into her pink Porsche.

"What's his name, girl?" Kenya asked.

"3Pac!!!" I said, crunk.

"Hell to the naw!" Kenya and Daja laughed, as we walked in the yard.

"Ride with me, girl. We gotta talk." Kenya confessed.

"K," I said, holding 3 Pac.

I slid into her still spanking new, yellow Maserati.

A gold Escalade, and a silver Escalade drove up.

"Detective Walker, and Officer Yorker," the dark skinned female detective said, introducing themselves, for what seemed like the three-thousandth time!

"I know who you are," I said.

"Pretty baby. He's gonna be a lady killa!" Miss Walker said.

I froze . . . Lady killer? 3 Pac? Oh, no . . . Lord, what have I gotten myself into to? Sleeping with the devil! Having a baby with the devil?

"Oh damn. Sorry girl. I didn't mean it like that," Detective Walker said, walking away smiling.

"Yea, De just silly, with her chocolate ass," The thick and nicely built, officer Jackson said.

"So, yall need us?" Kenya asked.

"No, Kenya PimpCity Brown, We're just glad and blessed to get Joe Brown down.", Miss Jackson said.

"Yall can go now," Miss Yorker said, and the three pretty cops walked into the nasty gruesome murder scene.

"Erica, I swear on my mama, he drugged my drink. We were all chilling and smoking. My man, Mr. Pimp City, came over with Joe. So I had my guards completely down. I left my glass of Grey Goose on the table. Then, I sat back down, and smoked with them. I started feeling funny, so I went to the bathroom again. I thought I had to throw up. I just stood over the toilet. Nothing."

"Baby! We gone!" Pimp yelled.

"So I came back out, and they were gone. Guuuurl, I felt insane and horny at the same time. I took all my clothes off, and slid down the pole, dancing and poppin' like a stripper. I was poppin' my big booty to that song, 'All I want for my birthday is a big booty gurl.' I started feeling extra freaky and dizzy. I started playing with myself. Gurl, I was laying on my back with my legs wide open. I just wanted to fuck. Anybody. I never felt so horny and hypnotized in my life."

"Then he walked in, and gave me some of his drink."

"Why are you naked?" Joe asked.

"I just laughed. I was geeked up. Where is Mr. Pimp City, I asked."

"He in the kitchen. Here, drink this," he said, giving me a glass.

"I took one non-stop deep swallow, and it was over with. I didn't even realize what I was doing"

"The next day, I was shaking my head, sitting naked on my bed. I played the whole thing out in my head. I knew he put a hot molly in my drink."

"Girl, that's heroin and cocaine. I'll never pop no pill. I don't care how many rappers and strippers say it's cool." I told Kenya.

I stared into her eyes, at the red light, while the a.c. blew hard in her yellow Maserati. Kenya never lied to me. Our eyes were locked on each other. She stared at me. A tear rolled down her right eye, and a tear rolled down my right eye.

"I believe you," I admitted.

"I love you, Erica," Kenya said, hugging me.

Beep! Beep!

"Move, slut! Get out the way!" a voice yelled behind us, from a van.

We forgot we were at the light!

Bang! Tap! Bang!

A huge, chocolate dude banged on the Maserati's yellow tinted window.

"Listen, you two dumb dike sluts. Me my wife and kids are trying to go to Georgia Aquarium. You hoes need to get the hell on and get a room!" he yelled.

Click.

Kenya stuck her red .44 in his mouth.

"Listen, fat fuck boy. I'm having a very bad day, and I may be feeling freaky, but I ain't gay. I'm pregnant, and don't know who's the father. I almost lost my best friend. I just killed a nigga I've known my entire life. Now, if you want to live to see them kids grow, and save your wife from fuckin a nigga named Joe, you better take your fat, black, undercover brotha, over-sized, gay, Godzilla-looking ass, back to that old ass, beat up van, before I blow your mother fucking tongue clean out the back of your head!" Kenya yelled.

Bam!

"Ha, ha. What's wrong, big boy? With your scary cat ass! Where's all that big mouth? Huh? Ok, oversized, wonder boy. Go back to your little family before I turn gay, and stick my shot gun up your scary big ass! Get!" I yelled, laughing.

Big boy pissed on himself! When Kenya PimpCity Brown had that thing in his mouth, you should have seen him! 3Pac was even laughing at his pissy butt! Fat boy was pissing and crying at the same damn time! Shakin' like a salt shaker!

Big boy ran to his van, with wet, blue, jogging pants, and his hairy butt crack showing!

"Ha, ha. Girl, you crazy! I thought you were gonna just blow his head off. I was not expecting the gangsta, female Scarface talk," I laughed.

Kenya looked at me with a chess game face, and drove off. "Ha, ha, girl. This ain't the day," my friend said, laughing and wiping a brand new tear from her face.

No lie, no lie. I felt so much better. No moe Joe! Plus, I got my best friend back! I always wanted it to be a dream. I'm glad he raped her. I mean, I know it's sad to cheer up on a rape, but I'm glad to know she was my friend. That bullet to his head, in front of his baby mamma, his sister, and his newborn, let me know.

She hated him, and he violated her. Damn!

Nicki Minaj ringtone . . .

I didn't even realized my phone was still on. I forgot I even grabbed it, but I answered.

"He's not dead."

"What?!" I asked.

"Joe Brown is not dead."

"But, he got shot in the head. I saw it with my own eyes!" I complained, wishing the ghost of this nigga would just die!

"He has a metal plate in his head, and he is in the custody of the Richmond County Police Department. They found drugs in his house, so he won't get out no time soon," the guy explained.

"Get out? What you mean, get out? Isn't he at least in a coma?" I asked stunned, feeling like a lion with no teeth, or a spider, with no web!

"No maam. He is very much alert."

Bloop!

I dropped the phone. My nightmare was still alive!

Screeech!

"Whoa! What the hell you doing?" Kenya asked, when I snatched the steering wheel, causing the car to slide to the end of the curb, through the opposite lane. Then, I slung it into park.

"I'm driving! I'm finna kill this nigga myself!" I yelled. I was pissed; hotter than a prostituted in Africa, with nothing but a leaf out-fit on!

"Do yo thang," Kenya said, getting out of the car, and allowing me to get into the driver's seat.

ZOOM. ZOOM. ZOOM.

I zipped past everybody in traffic. I was driving like a mixed kid; like I was mixed with fire truck and ambulance!

Yank. Yank.

I slung the Maserati into park, grabbed Kenya's pistol, and got out of the car.

"Watch my baby," is all I said, as I marched inside the hospital located in Augusta, GA.

"Excuse you!"

"Fuck you!" I told a gay, male nurse, pushing him out of my way.

"Fish patty!" the gay guy yelled.

Pow. I shot him right in the hospital, and kept walking, forcing my way onto a crowded elevator. I still had my gun in my hand, but no one noticed. Plus, I had out the silencer on the gun, right before I popped the nurse in the leg.

I had my red, Barbie girl wig on. My real hair was black as oil. No one would identify me. I would just bust this nigga five times in the head, and make sure he was dead!

The nurse would be fine. Hell, he was already a nurse. Nothing against gay people, I was just in my 'no bull-shit, kill zone.'

Boom!

I burst into his room, after asking the nurses at the nurses' station where the infamous Joe Brown was located.

"Drop your weapon!" Officer Walker said.

I wouldn't budge. I had my finger on the trigger, ready to kill a nigger!

"Miss Brown, drop the gun," Miss Walker said again.

I wasn't hearing jack! He was dying! Up close and personal! I ran up to the hospital bed, and aimed my gun.

"Dam!" I said, confused.

"He just left," the sexy, chocolate detective said.

"Where is he? What cat? I'll shoot the car up!" I told her.

"No. Too late. He is already in the jail by now. Sorry," Miss Walker said, looking at me, as if she felt my pain.

I was furious, and breathing hard like a track star. She gave me a big hug.

"It's ok, Erica. It's ok, baby. I've been there. I've been hit before. I been lied to. I've been abused. I've been cheated on, baby. Don't let this uniform fool you. There is a beautiful body, a real person, and a mother under this uniform. Put your gun away, and get out of here. Go out the back way, through the stairs. As a matter of fact, I'll walk you out. Twenty Richmond County officers are already here, looking for you. Watch the inmate for me, Miss Daniels. Follow me, Erica," Miss Walker said. "Turn around."

Click. Click.

She cuffed me, right after I dropped my red, curly wig. My real hair was black, and in a ponytail.

"You ain't trickin' me, and locking me up, are you?" I asked, thinking out loud.

Miss Walker didn't speak. She just continued to keep her composure. As always. She never showed emotion when she was upset.

The few times we met, she always had that First lady swagg. President's wife swagg. The chocolate Hillary Clinton. She was too cool to be a cop. She was built like a stripper; slim waist, round booty that jiggled with every step just like mine. She had short hair, and was air conditioned cool.

Click. Click.

"Get out of here," she told me, removing the hand cuffs.

"Thanks."

"Get in, fool," Kenya yelled, waving me down.

I ran and hopped in the Maserati, pimp ride. I saw all the cops, and ducked down, while I held 3Pac. I looked into my baby's eyes. That's when it hit me; hard like grits in the face of a cheating husband, or a whoopin' with a switch with thorns in it, against smooth legs!

My baby was staring into my eyes, smiling. His eyes were as red as Satan's. Did he have pink eye?

"Ka-ka," he giggled.

Oh Lord. I just shook it off.

"2 Pac back ... 2 Pac back ... That's what all these people screaming, that 2 Pac's back!" I rapped the Meek Mill song out loud. Me, Kenya, and baby 3 Pac all laughed at the same dang time!

Now that's the shitz I do like!

LOCK DOWN, JOE BROWN

Like a mummy, Joe Brown was wrapped up. He was sitting in Richmond County Jail, watching the news.

"The Atlanta Falcons are undefeated again! The best record in the NFL. 7 and 0," the news broadcaster, Rachael said.

"Hey mummy head, we don't watch no damn news up in here," a tall guy with dreds said.

Joe just looked at him. His entire face and head was wrapped up. He had been in the hospital several times and in the medical part of the jail as well. After six months, they finally cleared him to be in regular population. However, he was in no shape to argue or fight.

Bam!

Joe knocked him out like a stuffed dummy. "I love a nigga wit' dreds. You want to grow long hair like a slut, Ima drag you like I drag my slut," Joe said, grabbing the unconscious dude by his long hair, and pulling him to the door.

Joe surprised the scare crow hell out of dude when he quickly jumped up, and socked him dead in his nose.

Bam. Bam. Bam.

"Open the door, and get this trash, wit' his trash ass!" Joe shouted to the officers.

Everyone was shocked; officers and inmates.

"Wow, I mean, like, how did you do that?" Kenyatta, the first female officer, said.

The male officers drug the dude out of the dorm.

"Damn, a fighting mummy," Kenyatta said, laughing to her caramel home girl, Debra.

"Ha, ha. True. Mummy man went hard, girl," Debra said, while laughing, and hitting Kenyatta on the shoulder.

"Yall must not know who that is?" Ivory asked the other two female officers.

They both looked at her lost.

"That's Joe Brown," Ivory confessed.

"What?!" Kenyatta shouted.

"No!" Debra yelled

Wham!

The male officers slammed the door in Joe's face. When Joe turned around, fifteen niggas were cracking their knuckles.

"GD in here," Frankie said.

"Suwooo. Blood gang in here. Blood in, Blood out," Joe replied.

Frankie got in his face.

Bam! Joe dropped him like a pork skin on Muslim ground!

Bam! Wham! Pop! Boom!

"That's my gangsta!" Scotty yelled, catching Joe in the head, and knocking him against the door.

Now all the G's were ganging up on the handicapped gangsta. He was backing up, and fighting back.

Bam!

He knocked Mike out!

Bang!

"Got him!" D.J. Mac yelled after smacking Joe on the back with the T.V, laying him out on the ground.

"Down! Down!" The officers ran in, thirty deep, spraying pepper spray, and blinding everyone.

The inmates started choking. Joe was on the ground in excruciating pain.

"Pick this guy up, and carry him to medical. After that, lock him down," Lt. Neal told the officers.

"He's gonna be in a lot of trouble," female officer, Ivory said, out loud.

"No shit, that's why we're locking him down in a one man cell," Lt. Neal said.

"Damn, my head hurt," Joe said out loud, as he lay on the steel bed. He stayed in medical for a week. Now, he was in a one man cell, in deep pain. D.J. caught him with that T.V. His back was screaming in pain. His head felt like a high school band was marching in it.

"Joe Brown. Visitation," Officer Weaver said over the intercom.

"Come on, Brown. You got a visitor," the tall, light-skinned male officer informed him.

Officer Stockton escorted Joe to his visit. Joe looked the officer up and down, sizing him up, thinking about escape. Just knocking that nigga out, and putting on his uniform. Joe always knocked people out with his fist. He also took kick boxing for three years, and never lost a fight. So, he could also knock a man out with his legs!

Bang!

Joe looked up, startled. The thick door slammed in their faces before the officer could catch it.

Joe lit up, like a kid on Christmas, as soon as he walked through the sliding doors and saw me, his daughter, and his son. If you ever want to see a thug smile, visit him in jail! This was the biggest smile that I've ever seen on Joe's face, and I've known him all my life!

He grabbed the phone and smiled. "Damn, you look good. The kids getting so big! They are beautiful. CryMeka is adorable. CryMeka is the Beyoncé of all babies! And, little 3Pac is too cute and cool. Then, he look double tough! And you baby, Erica, damn, Erica. Turn around . . . Daaaamn (in his Martin voice)! That ass got phat! No waist. Pretty face, smooth skin. Damn! Looking good. You been working out?" He asked me, still standing up.

He looked better. Only his head was wrapped up. His face was completely healed. He had that handsome, young, baby face. I could tell he had been working out. The nigga muscles were ripped. I could see his chest print through his green V-neck shirt.

"Erica, I love you!" he shouted, putting his hands on the glass, waiting on me to open my palm out and pretend to be touching his hands.

I just looked at him, and shook my head. I looked at 3Pac. He was giggling. Then, I turned my attention to CryMeka, who was whining and irritated. Then, I sat down. I sat her on my lap, still holding 3Pac. Holding two babies is hard!

"Damn, boo, it's like that? My Red Ruby ain't got no love for daddy?"

Still no response.

"What the? Who brought you up here?" he asked.

I looked dead into his eyes.

"San and Trapp,"

"What?!" he roared like a lion in the jungle.

Bam!

He punched the fiberglass, cracking it.

"Damn you! Damn you! You think you can just handle me like this? Huh?! Huh?! Yeah. Ima kill you and your fake ass cousin! Just watch! F—you!" he yelled, then slammed the phone down. He walked away hot as a prostitute with a fireball in her couchie!

I laughed, and walked out with my babies.

"Freeze!"

When I got outside, five cops had their weapons aimed at Trapp and Santana.

Trapp and San had their weapons aimed too. Both of them had two, red .44 Magnums in each hand, ready to kill the cops. They had their backs to each other.

"What the?" I stuttered . . .

"Yall ain't touchin' my best friend! Yall gotta kill me too. Matter of fact, all yall drop your weapons, or I'll blow this whole damn street up! Blow the jail up too!" Mr. Pimp City said from his camouflage, bulletproof, army tank!

I'm holding my babies like "damn."

I would cover their eyes, but they won't remember this.

Mr. Pimp City spoke again from his 5,000 watt intercom.

"Drop your guns, or I'll blow everybody up! Kids, women, cops, and robbers. Play with me! 5,4,3,2 . . .1. Tic. Tic . . ."

"Disarm! Disarm!" Detective Walker ordered, from her red Benz. She was hanging out of the red tinted window with her intercom in her hand.

"Thought so. Erica, get in," Pimp City told me and my kids.

I looked at him, thought about it, then changed my mind.

"Erica, you and the kids get in," Miss Walker said.

Zoom!

"Get in," Kenya said, racing up to me, stomping on her brakes, hard. She pulled up right beside me and the kids, and Miss Walker.

"What is this? Save Erica day?" I asked, laughing.

"Trick, get in," Kenya said, looking serious and anxious. I could tell she was ready to disappear from this situation.

I decided to jump in with her, and ride out. Trapp and San went on a high speed chase with the cops.

Mr. Pimp City more than saved Trapp and San's lives. Because just as sure as scrambled eggs, pig guts, and fart stinks. Trapp and Santana were shooting at them cops! They were not giving in to the law. Under no circumstances. It was death or escape, nothing else. Hopefully, they had escaped.

Mr. Pimp City slowly drove away in his army tank, in the opposite direction. A helicopter, and eight cars followed Pimp, and twenty cars chased Trapp and San.

Stop...

Pimp City stopped the tank in the middle of the street. The cops had the tank completely surrounded.

This had now made worldwide news. Every T.V. station on earth was watching. The Mr. Pimp City army tank/police stand-off. Mr. Pimp was not moving. The cops feared the dynamite that Miss Walker had warned them about. She knew about Mr. Pimp City's deadly explosives. She stood in the street, in midst of the crowd. No one knew for sure that Mr. Pimp City was the driver, except for me and the crew. Miss Walker, just had a hunch that it was him.

"Any ID on the driver?" FBI Agent, Allen asked.

"Yeah, I'm guessing, it's the living legend, Mr. Pimp City, from Candler Rd," Miss Walker said, guessing out loud.

"OK. Did you see him?" the man asked.

"No."

"Do you recognize his voice?"

"No."

"Oh, have you seen his tank before?"

"No," she answered, never blinking, emotionless, arms folded, standing by her car, eyes locked on the tank like superglue.

"Well how in the corndog hell, do you know who is driving the damn army tank? You don't recognize his face, and you never saw the army tank. Did you fuck the suspect?"

Slap!

"Watch yo mouth, boy," Miss Walker said, back slapping the Juicy Fruit chewing gum right out of FBI Special Agent Allen's smart mouth.

Still, her eyes stayed straight on the tank, never blinking. Of course, she didn't know for sure who was in that tank. But she knew her area. She knew the history of Atlanta and Decatur. She knew who had the power in the street. She knew every known drug dealer and gang member in each zone; from zone 1 through six. She knew who had the money and the power. Even though Miss Walker couldn't prove it, she knew, without a doubt in do-do hell, that that army tank belonged to Mr. Pimp City, A.K.A. Earl the Pearl Brown.

"Ok, this stand-off has lasted twenty-four hours. Blow up the tank," Mr. Riles ordered.

KahBoom! Boom! Boom!

Deafening, loud, hard explosions.

The missiles completely destroyed the tank. Ten missiles blew a hole in the concrete road that was ten feet deep, eighty inches wide. The tank was gone like 2012.

Claps. Applause. Loud police celebration.

Rachael was live, giving the play by play scoop of the entire incident. People were, watching, cheering at home, and in bars. Of course, the boys in the hood cheered for the bad guys.

"Yeeaaay! We got him! Blown to smithereens!" Lt. Neal said. He and Srg. Beard gave each other high fives.

"Dee! Dee! We got that sucker, and the two other clowns in the county jail!"

Srg. Beard cheered to Detective Walker. However, she didn't blink, sweat, or even crack a smile.

"What now? Why aren't you celebrating? We killed the bad guy!" Lt. Neal shouted, shaking her shoulders.

"Stop. Stop shaking me. I'm just not impressed," Miss Walker said, and walked away. This time, Chief Detective Walker hopped into her money green Porsche with the platinum steering wheel and custom design rims to match.

"Somethin' ain't right about her," Neal said.

"Umph."

"Shut up, 'cause even you was staring. EVERYTHING is right about that butt!" Beard said laughing, hitting Neal in the stomach, as they watched her butt shake and giggle in her slacks. She had a small waist, and Walker walk-so sexy. A bo-legged cop. She knew she was the finest chocolate girl on the planet. Quickly, she spun around and look at them mean and hard.

"Hah!"

They both jumped, then held their heads down in shame. Detective Walker caught them red-handed pointing, staring, and laughing at how fine her round, voluptuous behind was.

"Yeah, whatever!" she said in a low voice, pulling off, while listening to Beyoncé. Their tongues were still out; they were drooling everywhere!

WHAT GOES UP, MUST COME DOWN

I was chillin' like a villain.

Knock. Knock. Knock.

"Who da hell is it?" I walked to the door carrying my son on my right hip, and opened the door.

"Hey Miss Brown," Secret Agent Washington and Chief Agent Yorker of the FBI said, greeting me.

"This house had been seized. It was purchased with illegal funds and will be foreclosed. This house, along with the other five houses, two mansions, the barber shop, the beauty salon in your name, all twenty-five of yall vehicles, the apartment, and the town house in your name. So, neither you nor Mr. Joe Brown owns any property as of now," the tall, dark, female FBI agent said.

"To make a long story short, drug money, baby," the brown-skinned FBI agent, Miss Yorker said, while smiling and winking her eye.

"Bietch, what's funny?" I asked the smart-mouthed, big-booty po-po.

"Slut, what's funny is you ain't got no money!" Miss Yorker said, and walked into my used-to-be five bedroom house.

I held my son a little tighter, and bounced up and down on my tippy toes.

"Fine, I'm Gucci. I got family in Saint Louis," I said out loud.

"Great, so tell Nelly and dem to come pack your shit. You got twenty-four hours, or you and your babies will be looking like a real, broke, Saint Lunatic!" the smart-mouthed Yorker said again, laughing out loud.

"Yea, laugh . . . I bet you Erica Hustle-N-Flow Brown won't stay down. Matter of fact, you can have all this shit! All twenty houses, thirty cars, and the bike! Stick it up your funky, female, FBI couchie!" I yelled, then left started to leave with my babies.

"Hopeless, hoe," Yorker added, like she wanted to fight.

"Fuck it. You wanna fight?" I asked her.

"Yea, come on. You think Joe Brown beat you down, slut, Ima beat the black off ya brain, you black, plastic Barbie, two bastard baby-having ass!" Yorker growled, in my face.

I put my son down.

Bam!

"Nobody talks about my kids"! I kicked her dead in the head.

"Don't hold her! I'm good!" Yorker yelled to Washington.

Bam!

"Whoa, nice one!" The slut must have known karate too, 'cause she kicked me in the right titty, causing me to stumble over my baby girl and fall.

Bam! Bam! Miss. Drop!

She stomped twice, I rolled out of the way, grabbed her legs, and snatched her on the ground with me. Then I got on top of her.

Pssss.

"Dammit!" I coughed like hell. That slut sprayed me.

"Chill. Chill. This ain't the Fine Female Wrestlers of WWE. Cut it out! Be professional! Leave it up to black folks. We gotta show our color," Detective Walker said, again on the scene.

I thought about it. She was right, as always. She was like my personal, police, guardian angel.

I looked at myself. I was actually fighting in thongs and a bra! Looking like a boxing stripper, on mud night. Thongs showing all of my curves, and Miss Yorker had on a black Victoria Secret bra. We looked like two fine strippers on Magic City Monday.

"Ha, ha." We both laughed at each other, shook hands, and separated.

"Get in," Kenya said, coming to my rescue, again.

Yeah, she proved to be a dependable friend. My doubts were gone; she is too legit to quit!

"Yall can stay with me."

"Naw, we Gucci. Take me to my mama's house," I told her, reminiscing about mama's too delicious, Saint Louis, cooking.

"How is Miss Joyce doing, anyway?" Kenya asked.

I just looked at her.

"Oh, she still mad about the Joe thing?" Kenya asked, already knowing the answer.

"Yea, but she mad at you, not him. Or should I say, disappointed. Damn him!" I snapped.

The Nikki Minaj ringtone came on. I accepted the call.

"Hey baby, I been thinkin. When I get out, I'm changing my life. No more drugs, crime, or violence. I'm changin' my life. Goin' to church. Maybe speak to kids—"

"Listen nigga, ain't no damn next time. I don't care if you own three churches! You destroyed my relationship with my twin sister, my best friend, my mother, and my brother! I be damned if I allow you to beat me and cheat me, in front of my kids! Nigga, I hope you rot in that slut! I don't give a fuck! I been giving my pussy to nobody but Joe Brown. Joe Brown, Joe Brown, Joe Brown. Muther fuck, Joe Brown! You ain't holding me down! I don't give a damn if D.J. hit you in the head with ten more TV's, a VCR, and a breakfast tray! I'm through with you, nigga! I hate you, nigga! Nigga, Ima give Trapp this pussy. Your cousin, shit somebody! Nigga, I might just fuck your sister, since you fucked mine! Daja is kinda cute. You gone pay!"

"God forgive me for cussing, but I been waiting years for this. Nigga, its Hurricane Erica and Volcano Brown! I'm ripping and burning everything down. You don't have shit! No cars, no houses, no wife, and no kids! You a dog, nigga! And it payback time, Joe Brown! It's Erica's time to shine now, nigga!"

"Click!" Kenya said, extra loud, laughing, as I hung up on him.

I was through crying. I washed my soft hands, and my pretty feet. I was through with this nigga. It was over! The fat lady, the fat baby, and the fat man had sang! It was over!

"Where you wanna go?"

"Kenya, boo, take me to my mom's."

"You sure you don't want to chill with your right hand chick?"

"Ha, ha. Naw, bae. I love you, but I need to spend some time with my mom and family. I was so caught up on that nigga that I forgot about my blood. We only live once. We have to show the ones that really love us that we also love and appreciate them."

I looked at Kenya. She had tears in both eyes.

"I love you, Erica. I really do . . ." she said, crying.

"I love you, too." I hugged her, while we sat in front of my mom's car.

Tap. Tap.

"Uhhh!" I jumped.

"Hey, Mama Brown."

"Hey, Kenya. Glad to see you two together, and not falling out over that no good ass man. Dicks are like dimes. You can get them anytime!" mom said.

We all laughed hella hard.

"Love you, Miss Brown."

"Love you too, child. You been my little pookey pooh, since your curly head butt was born. Now get in here and get some of mama's corn bread, sweet potato pie, mashed potatoes, collard greens, fried chicken, and ghetto red, super sweet, Kool-Aid!" mama said, laughing.

"Mmmmmmm," me and Kenya both agreed.

Dinner was so delicious. Nothin' like mama's good ole', Saint Louis style dinner!

I enjoyed being with my entire family. Kenya was laughing at mama's truthful joking. Porsche was chewing away. Bre'Shauna was helping Crymeka eat. Uncle Chicago and Uncle O.G. Hood was sipping beer and talking sports with Dog Man, who was free again. Aunty Liz, my mom's baby sister, was laughing and talking to her son, Buster. My cousin Devin was feeding her twins. Aunty Danika, was joking with Aunty Melinda about the time they cut Uncle Cordell's afro while he was sleeping!

"Erica, girl, I'm so glad I got to see you again, before I went back to Minnesota in the morning," Aunty Melinda said.

"Me too, Aunty. I miss you coming down here. And Saniya is getting big!" I said, shocked at the size of her adorable, ten year old daughter.

Saniya was too cute, rapping with her little sister, Asia. They were pretending the chicken leg was a microphone.

"Surpriiiise!" a voice yelled in my ear.

I turned around, and my nineteen year old niece, Destiny was holding a chocolate cake with my name on it.

"Happy Birthday, Erica!!!!" everyone yelled simultaneously.

Hot dam of Sam! All this drama, and I forgot it was my birthday!

"Make a wish, Aunty," my nephew, Carnell said.

"No moe Joe!" I yelled, then blew the candles out.

"Ha, ha!!!" everyone laughed, clapped, and cheered.

FUNNY HOW TIME FLIES

Crymeka was six years old, 3Pac was five, and super live! I had been living with my mom, and working as a correctional officer. I never went to see Joe again. Damn that nigga. I had moved on. However, I had to profess to the world, that I was as broke as a penny with two holes in it.

"Dang!" I shouted, after checking my mailbox. "One, two, three, four, five, six, seven, eight, nine, ten, fifteen, twenty, thirty-five letters from this nigga! What the hell!"

I scratched my head. This idiot had written me two-hundred letters a week, for four years straight. I never responded to one. Today, I decided to respond, with a picture.

"Hey you, come 'ere!" I yelled to a teenage boy with a mo-hawk, walking by in skinny jeans.

"What up, shawty?" he said, ATL, country to death.

I called my nephew out of the house. "Nephew! Carnell, take this picture for me," I told my nephew.

"What up, shawty?" the dude asked.

"Shut up and come here." I grabbed my seventeen year old, A-town shawty, and stuck my tongue on his tongue.

Snap. He took the picture.

I had on some extra-short boy shorts. You could see my entire cheeks. They were so tight, you could see my skin through the thongs. The, white boy shorts were cutting up my butt crack.

Snap.

"Ok, thanks."

"Damn, can I get yo number?!"

"Ha, ha," I laughed.

"Bietch!"

Bam!

Before I could think, I kicked that nigga front teeth out, with a right-sided karate kick.

Cha ching!

Two gold teeth fell out!

"Thank you, Aunty. I got a new pinky ring," my silly nephew Carnell joked.

"Too silly," I laughed.

Crunch.

I stepped on this disrespectful jerk's head, and hopped on my aunty Quitta's lime green motorcycle. I zoomed to Walgreens to develop the pictures for Joe.

"Mail call!" Officer Brunson announced, inside the Billy Goat State Prison in middle Georgia.

Billy Goat was the name of an eighteen year old white girl, who killed two billy goats with a ping pong ball, changed her name to Billy Goat, and then served as the mayor for four years! The prison was named after, Ooops, she died while choking on billy goat meat on Thanksgiving Day! "Oh well, what goes around, comes around," is all her son, Willie Goat, could say, after he cried like a baby.

"Bietch! Ima kill her!" Joe shouted.

"Hell naw! Ain't that your so-called, faithful, virgin, baby-mama?" T-Bone said.

Joe knocked him out, and ripped the pictures of me up. He was furious. He didn't have any money on his books. All the girls he had, ignored him like a tore up, funky, shower shoe.

Joe Brown was down. Broke with no hope. Revenge was on his mind.

Bang!

He slammed his cell door.

Kick! Kick! Pop! Boom! Drop! Plop! Bang!

His cellmate was laying on his paper thin mattress on the floor, reading Real Life Action.

Joe gave him real life action, kicking him straight in the head twice, and then hitting him in the back with a small New Testament Bible. Joe then picked the two-hundred and eighty pounder up, and threw him into the wall. He sent him flying across the cell. Joe punched him twice, splitting his eyes open, like a couchie. He dragged him by the legs, and left him outside of the cell door.

"Joe Brown, visitation."

Joe was as shocked as a cat cornered by a bull dog.

He was always fresh. He shaved real quick. His hair was already lined up, as perfect as a professional drawing. He knew it was his baby mama. He nervously walked out of the dorm, and into the visitation room.

"Hey baby," Joe said, looking at me with a funny question mark on his face.

"Hey," I said as plain as a number two pencil.

"Why you ain't wrote me back? Where are my kids? Damn, you getting pretty fat," he said, waiting on me to hug him.

I sat down.

"I'm never writing you, again. My kids are with their stepfather, Pimp—"

"Pimp?! What the hell, and why the hell you try me with them pictures?" he roared.

"Joe, shut the hell up, before I leave your broke, hopeless, ex-ballin', no hoe havin' ass in this visitation room! AND nigga, I'm two months pregnant by a officer at this prison. Any more questions, punk?" I shined.

Joe was fire red. Like three-hundred firecrackers on the Fourth of July. He stared straight into my soul. No lie, my heart skipped a beat. My feet were glued to the ground. I couldn't move.

"Oh yeah, yeah. Everybody wanna kick Joe Brown when he down. Erica, you will pay. Believe that."

"Pay?! Nigga, the only thing Ima pay you is no attention. You had my sister, best friend, strippers, and had a baby on me. You cheated and beat on me. Nigga, I don't feel sorry for you. You kidnapped me, and fed me noodles. Nigga—"

Twah.

I spit in his face.

"Bietch!" He jumped up, and grabbed my neck.

"No! No! Brown, stop!" Officer Jamison yelled, charging at Joe with Officer Story and five more officers.

Wham!

They tackled Joe, handcuffed him behind his back, and sprayed him.

"Dog!"

They piled on top of him, like a high school, football team!

Whoooa!

Pap! Pap! Pap!

Out of nowhere, Joe popped up, like a jack in the box. He knocked out two male officers, and a female; all with right handed punches.

Damn, he still had it!

Then, he charged at me, like a serial killing vampire on crack.

Wham!

Surprise. I met him with a size five in his eyes!

Woosh.

That nigga slid like a kid.

Twah.

I spit on Joe Brown, the clown, again.

Whack! Whack!

Jamison and the rest of the officers clobbered him with their sticks. Now it was ten on one. They were giving him a down south, Mississippi slave, butt whippin'! Blood was pouring out like a water fountain. They yanked his hands behind his back, and cuffed him, Georgia prison style!

He was bleeding, and looking pitiful. I laughed, showed him my pregnant stomach, and rubbed my baby.

"See ya next lifetime. Bout to do a threesome wit Trapp. Ha, ha," I laughed.

"Hell naw!" Officer Story laughed.

"Biit—"

Whack! Smack!

Jamison wouldn't even let him get the b-word all the way out of his bloody mouth! I blew him a kiss, and shot him the bird at the same dang time.

REVENGE IS LIKE THE SWEETEST JOY!

They dragged the fighting, kicking, Joe Brown back to his cell.

Blunk!

They tossed him on the floor, and Jamison took off the handcuffs.

"Umph."

He kicked him with his Vaseline shinny boots, one last time. Then Jamison left the felon/former street soldier, on the cement floor in pain.

Click. Click.

The cell door opened and closed.

"Well, well, well, Joe Brown," a familiar voice said, like the ghetto grim reaper, dressed in all black with A-town gold teeth!

Joe shook. Then bucked his eyes wide open, and closed them again, hoping he was dreaming.

"Yeah nigga, it's me. Your worst nightmare, monkey nigga! It's Santana!" San said.

Even though Joe was already down for the count and defenseless, San didn't have one inch of sympathy for him.

"Nigga, no! No! Don't punk out on me now, nigga. You got a kick out of beating on a female. You got a kick out of knocking my little cousin teeth out, shooting her, breakin' her arm, raping her sister, raping her best friend, kidnapping her, getting her beat up at church, and nearly thrown in jail, after giving birth. Nigga, I'm about to beat yo' punk ass for old and new!"

"Let me hit 'em," Lil Nath said.

"Let me kick 'em," N.O. added.

"Let me eat this hoe too!" Summer Hill chipped in.

"Naw. Give me the first five minutes. Then yall mob in, and beat this hoe until he ain't breathing!" San demanded.

Click.

They closed the door.

San gave a happy, evil, satisfied, grin.

Snap.

He took a picture with his three-hundred year old, Verizon flip phone that he snuck in.

"That's before Erica. Wait till you see the after picture!"

Joe could only lay there on his stomach, and move his eyes.

Bam. Bam. Bam. Klonk. Klonk. Stomp. Bimp. Boom. Lick. Knee. Cussing. Slapping. Kicking up the butt. Stomp. Jumping on his head with two feet. Yeeeeeee!

Santana leaped off the steel bed, and landed on Joe's stiff, frozen, bloody head.

"Tag in. Finish."

"Mob life or no life," Dirty said. Dirty was the head Mob member in the Middle, G.A. Prison.

"YMF and GF style," Black Child added. The other fierce fighting ATL MOB leader from the city boasted.

"Let the beating begin!" John A.K.A Summer Hill added.

Santana walked away, smiling. "Take a picture when it's over," San told the Atlanta Mob.

Nikki Minaj ring back . . .

"Hello?" I answered, getting a full body massage for the first time in my life, by a man that was tall, dark, and lovely.

"Cuz, be on stand-by."

"Awe, that feels so good . . . Oh! Stand by for what, cuz?" I asked, still mesmerized by the big, strong, professional, and delicate, massaging hands of the black king on my tender skin.

"Revenge is the sweetest joy, next to getting' p . . . Words of the late, great Tupac," he said, then hung up.

"Damn!" I almost caught a heart attack, when I received those two pictures!

"Who da hell is this ugly, disgusting faced dude? He got a skinny skeleton, worm eating, bloody windshield, car crash, hammer hitting, burnt-up skin, plastic surgery, three degree burnt, hog intestines face!" I said, scared.

Clunk!

I tossed the phone on the cold floor.

"Pay back is a slut, cuz, . . ." I heard San say, before he sent the picture message. That's when it hit me. Boom! Hard like a pregnant hurricane!

My eyes were eagle wide. My voice was gone. I covered my wide open mouth with my pretty hands. Joe looked worse than any human's face I had ever seen. Unreal . . . Unhuman.

I forced myself up, and slowly walked to the phone, looking around as if I was sneaking to steal cookies form grandma. Then, I bent over, and picked up the phone. Next picture.

"Umph,"

Unbelievable. They put his entire bloody body inside of a clear, large, trash bag! The bag was so bloody, it looked synthetic! It looked like someone poured ten gallons of red paint in the trash bag with Joe's body, and tossed it to the Hulk, to shake the bag up like some dice!

Clunk! Clunk!

I threw the phone back down, and A-town stomped it with my brand new, baby blue, Carolina Jordans! Excuse my violation to the Blood Gang, but these Carolina Blue Jays go hard!

I laughed, and hopped into my one-thousand dollar, cheap, silver, Honda.

I thought about all the dirt Joe Brown had done to me. Was I happy? Hmmmmmmm.

ROUND AND ROUND WE GO

"Hey! Joe Brown pack yo stuff, boy. You transferring," Srg. Riles said.

Knock. Knock.

He knocked on his bunk bed.

"Boy?" Joe stretched and mumbled in his sleep.

"Get up, Brown. Have all your property ready, I'll be back at 3 AM. To get you," Srg Riles said. Every Tuesday and Thursday mornings were transfer days in the G.A. prison.

Joe survived a very fatal butt whooping and attempted murder. Srg. Riles saved his life when Captain Pope spotted the commotion, and sent Riles in to save the day.

Joe's throat had been cut. They cut both of his ankles with a razor, broke his nose, jaw, and hand. Joe had actually died, but nurse Joiner revived him back to life. Muwah . . . with a mouth to mouth kiss. Then, Mr. Brown started breathing again. Mob boss, Dirty, had chocked him out.

However, four months later, he was back on his feet, and transferring to another prison. Warden Holloway refused to let Joe Brown back on the prison compound.

His prison files let her know that he would surely seek revenge on one of his adversaries. It was a long, awkward, uncomfortable ride to Jacksonville, G.A.

A lot of niggas told each other jail house lies and fake, prison war stories. Some true, but only five percent of them.

Like the time Polo took a broom, and beat ten niggas in the head, in the hardest prison in GA, called Alto. Or when Pimp City fought fifteen gang members who all had knives, in D-building at V.D. State prison, by himself, and Pimp never hit the ground! Those were the only true prison stories out of the five-hundred he had heard.

"Wake up! Crenshaw State Prison Bay!" the transfer officer announced.

Joe's eye got bigger than a tarantula's booty hole when he saw it!

"Come off that bus, inmate! Kick this one in the ass! He look like one of those city slickers! We hate Atlanta niggers in South Georgia, boy! Just 'cause yall got Monica and that damn Waka Flocka, yall think yall the shit!"

"Beat his ass!" I ordered the five, six-foot, two-hundred and ninety five pound cert Team officers.

The Cert Team was dressed in all black, carrying pepper spray and sticks. You shoulda seen the look on Joe Brown's face when he saw me! I climbed up in rank inside the prison to become Lieutenant. So, I was pretty much my own boss, with boss status! My cousin, Porsche was the warden, so I specifically asked to be here when his ass arrived.

Dah! Dong! Ding! Ding! Boom!

He still had the iron leg cuffs around his ankles. The big guys immediately snatched him down the steps, off the bus. They busted him in the back of the head, when he made it to the bottom step.

Woosh! Bang!

Two of the giant Cert Team members snatched him by his legs onto the concrete, cracking the other part of his head.

"Hey, Eri . . ."

Boot-in the face!

I politely stomped his throat before he could yell my name.

"Behave yourself, you disrespectful inmate! You want to jump on our officers, threaten the warden at the other prison, and rape nurses?! Not at my camp! Beat this worthless inmate until he change colors! Make him look like a bag of sour cream chips!" I told my Cert Team; my beat a inmate down, crew.

They picked him up, tossed him two feet in the air, and watched him in fast, slow motion. Bang! Crack!

"Ouch! Damn!"

He landed on his back.

Stomp! Kick! Stomp! Stomp! Stomp!

They kicked that boy to sleep, then kicked him back awake! The other twenty inmates that came on the bus were standing in a straight line, in attention, stiff as a disciplined military platoon! They probably thought each of them were next. They were all defenseless, in handcuffs and leg irons.

"Stop! Enough!" a strong voice demanded.

Whoa! Everyone turned around. It was Trapp and forty four Bloods, gang prisoners. They all had on grey sweaters and black skull caps.

"What the hell?!" the tallest Cert member said.

Trapp and the forty four Bloods surrounded the five huge officers.

The big officers were now nervous and sweating like seals!

All forty four of Trapp's Blood brothers had super sharp knives in each hand. Trapp had a seventeen inch lawnmower blade, as huge as a sword, and razor sharp. The blade was sharp enough to slice off an elephant's head-Bushwick's special sharp knife! Joe was laying on the concrete, motionless. Trapp kicked him to see if he was alive. He wiggled one leg for a second. Trapp spoke like a calm, cool, intelligent kid. Of course he was the National Chess Champion on the street, but shot four niggas in the parking lot, after winning the chess trophy! He shot him for staring at him the wrong way.

Pow!

"Listen. Either yall leave my dog alone, or every single officer at this prison dies. One by one. The National Guards will have no choice but to detonate the entire prison, because we will not surrender. He is one of ours. No Blood will bleed blood, unless it's by a Blood. Blood in, Blood out. We will punish our own," Trapp announced like the Blood gang President, serious as death.

"Leave him alone. Take him to medical," female Captain Cedra ordered.

The Cert Team picked up his bloody, beat-up, bruised body.

"No," Usef yelled. "We got him."

Four Bloods carried him to medical. The gang was forty-five deep!

"How long can we keep Joe Brown at this prison?" Lt. Joiner asked me while she sat behind her desk, playing with a Metro touch screen she found hidden in an inmate's cell.

"Why?"

"Look Erica, that's your baby's daddy. People know you are seeking retribution for all the evil Joe Brown did to you. Of course, he is no black Robin Hood. But someone in Atlanta will soon find out. Some dumb inmate will snitch on you for a transfer, or to gain brownie points with warden, Porsche. We can't keep him here any longer. I think we should transfer him Thursday," Lt. Joiner stated.

"I say, damn you, Kenyatta! That nigga will get beat up every day, until I say stop! When Atlanta transfers him to another prison, I will transfer with him! If they find out that I'm his baby mama, I will come visit him, and cut his damn throat, trick! That nigga shot me, broke my arm, kidnapped me, raped my best friend and my sister, knocked my teeth out, and had me beat up at church-with my brand new born baby! Damn Joe Brown and you, and whoever don't like it. It's payback time, mother fucker! And Joe pays! It's Erica Brown's time to shine now!" I yelled, not realizing I was right smack in her face, bending over the desk, with my nose touching her nose.

"Whatever, honey. Keep that up, and yo black ass will be in prison with Joe Brown's ass! Ha, ha," Lt. Joiner laughed.

"Damn Joe!" I said, then stormed out of the office with an evil twist in my hips. Still super sexy though.

"How is he?" I asked nurse Leslie.

"Not looking good, but he'll heal."

Whap!

"Hey, you can't do that," nurse Leslie said, after I smacked Joe in the mouth, knocking out the same two side teeth that he once knocked out of my mouth.

That flashlight was hella hard!

I looked her up and down.

"If you got a problem wit' it, see me after work. And if you lookin' for me, I'll be in Decatur, hoe! I'm taking these teeth with me," I said sticking the two teeth in my bra, walking off, eyeballing her, and not even giving her the joy to lust at my phat, fine behind!

"C.O.'s are so dirty," she told the silent killer.

Joe stayed in the medical section on 2b for two weeks.

"Mr. Brown, you heal fast. Why did you get jumped on. Why does every officer at the prison hate you? Is it because of that trick, Lt. Brown? The one that all the men want to screw, just because she got a phat ass, long hair, smooth brown skin, and a beautiful face and smile?" nurse Leslie said, just staring at Joe Brown.

Joe looked the tall, yellow, pretty nurse, up and down. She was gorgeous. They gave Joe fifteen years, he had already pulled five. He could parole in another year or two. It hit him.

"Yea. Can you help me?" he asked, regaining his charm.

He stared deep into the nurse's eyes. His eyes hypnotized her. She froze . . .

Then, she shook it off.

"Oh well, do she know you, personally?"

"I guess. She my baby momma-,"

"Stop! I got a plan. Get one of your boys with a phone tomorrow to record her ordering you to get beat up, and BINGO! Law suit, baby! You get out!" she yelled quietly.

"And Bingo! You rich, 'cause I don't want no money, I just want the hoe dead."

"I want the money . . . Oh, and your freedom too."

Joe stayed in medical another week. He got very cool with the yellow-boned nurse.

"Yeah, nigga! Blatt! Blatt! Joe Brown back on the set niggas! Get at me!" Joe yelled, pounding his chest like a pretty boy King Kong. He made an announcement when he first entered the open dorm.

There were mostly Bloods in dorm fourteen, but none of them uttered a word.

"What? What? Yall ain't fucking with Joe Brown campaign? Huh?" Joe said again.

The dorm held ninety inmates, seventy of them Bloods, fifteen Muslims, and the rest, normal, civilian inmates.

Joe didn't have any weapons. He knew he didn't violate. But he also knew that I was a Blood. So I could have easily spread a rumor, to his dirty name.

"Hey, the police say you a rat!" Skooter confessed, to break the silence.

The double bunk beds were lined up in sections. Five bunk beds in each cut, separated by a small brick wall.

The three T.V.'s were in an open day room area. All seventy Bloods had Joe surrounded.

"You calling Joe Brown a snitch? Really? Yall niggas crazy. So what? Yall gone eat me? Huh? Yall niggas wanna eat Joe Brown? I'm on the plate with no proof. Well, I'm ready to die, nigga!" Joe yelled.

Woof!

A thick notebook tablet hit the floor right in front of his feet.

"What the hell is this crap?" Joe asked, picking up the notebook. Then, he started flipping through it.

"Evidence," Skooter stated.

"Nigga, I'm 9 Trey, all day, every day. This ain't my handwriting. So my baby mama done brain washed yall fools?" Joe questioned, waiting for sympathy. He looked at the crowd. No one believed him. He was considered food on the plate, and was about to get ate.

He looked in everyone's eyes, then he spotted me, standing outside the dorm. I waved at him, and blew him a kiss.

"Bye, Bye, nigga! Blatt!" I barked.

Boom! Boom! Boom!

They rushed him. The first thing he did was grab Skooter, and hold him while they stomped him.

"Hold that nigga! Move! I'm tryna stick him!" Money said, waving them out of the way so that he could ram the six inch shank (prison knife) in his spine.

Ziiiiif!

Money stabbed him in the back.

Boom! Kick! Stomp! Stomp! Kick! Kah Booooom!

Two niggas slammed a six foot tall, ten inch wide, metal locker on his back!

Boom!

Miami and Vine City dove on top of the locker.

Crack! They broke his back!

"12! 12!" they yelled.

Twelve meant the police were coming. Supreme stood across in the other dorm, and watched the entire episode. There were four dorms, two on each side. They could see into the two dorms, that faced each other.

"10! 10!."

"10! 10!"

The officers' radios were going off, loud!

Thirty officers ran into the dorm.

"Ah! At! Achew!" inmates sneezed and coughed, and covered their eyes, as they spread out like fish, from the strong, stinging pepper spray.

Once again, Joe Brown got beat down, badly.

"Paralyzed from the neck down. Spinal damage at the top of his neck, in the back," Nurse Melinda said.

"Excellent," I said, and walked out of Savannah State Hospital.

"Bingo!" Nurse Leslie cheered, as soon as she watched the entire catastrophe on her phone. She had everything! This white, chubby dude, named Terrell, caught it all on video!

I stood in the window, smiling, while watching the entire fight unfold, instead of following protocol and getting on my radio to call the code.

The video revealed that the moment I yelled, "Blatt!," the Bloods attacked Joe. This proved I ordered the hit. A tall, light-skinned guy named Mr. Render, was the only one attempting to stop it. There was no hope for Joe.

However, there was no hope for me, either; not to keep this job! Plus, Nurse Leslie was headed to Grady to pull the birth certificates for my kids, to prove Joe Brown was the father. They would press charges on me for conspiracy to murder. Federal time! This would be huge news.

Everyone would go down; from the warden, Porsche, who was my cousin, on down to Ashley, my friend, working the control booth, and allowed this to transpire.

They had to fly Joe to Atlanta Medical. He was barely breathing, and had to immediately receive a blood transfusion. Nurse Leslie was licking her lips in the parking lot.

Bam!

Leslie turned around, she was just about to open her car door.

"What you got in your hand, trick?" I asked the tall, yellow bone.

Lie sign number one-when a person who doesn't usually stutter, immediately starts stuttering.

"Umm, mmm, I, I, ain't got no, nothing," she lied, avoiding eye contact.

I was not moving. I stared straight into her soul.

Bang!

I smacked the nursing knowledge out of her head with my giant, Joe beating flash light.

Her body went limp. I took her purse, and jumped into my beat up Honda.

I knew she had the fight recorded. That would end my cop career. Like I really gave a damn! I missed the lifestyle of the drug game. No lie. I was tired of being broke, working from check to check. I started to feel half way decent about this bad luck that I was bringing to Joe.

"Ha, ha," I smiled, shaking up his two teeth that I knocked out.

"Blatt!" I yelled on the video. Yeah, nice video. I watch the entire beat down of Joe Brown again, and enjoyed it.

Nurse Leslie did an excellent job. Too bad I, bang! broke the evidence with my flashlight.

Woosh! Toosh!

I pulled off the road, and tossed the phone into the lake, then I drove home.

Joyce Brown, and Kenya PimpCity Brown were standing in the front yard with Lewis, from Summerhill.

"Ima just charge yall fifteen dollars to cut the grass, and a dub of Keysha to smoke on."

"No! You can't smoke on me, for free," Keysha said, coming out of the house, wearing white, tight, boy shorts and a wife beater, and no bra, exposing her nipples. She was ghetto foxy fine; identical to me, and had the exact same booty that I had. My two kids gave me the extra juice in my booty.

Lewis looked at Keysha and laughed. "I'll cut the grass for free, for you," he told her.

She looked at her camel toe. "I need my grass cut too."

Lewis choked.

She grabbed him by the hand, and led him into the back yard. His back was against the house. She was in his arms, tongue kissing him, while he gripped her rump like no tomorrow. His legs buckled when she toyed with her tongue ring-inside his ears, down his neck, and then slid it back into his mouth.

Dang! He was brick man, mason hard!

They both closed their eyes. She was ocean, lake, river wet.

"Mama!"

"Huh?"

They both turned around, shocked!

Her nephew was on the ground, yelling as loud as a last second, winning, Super bowl touchdown by the Atlanta Falcons!

God! I took off running to the backyard when I heard my five year old son hollering. Mom and Kenya were right behind me! I beat Keysha to him, and she was already back there!

"Ah."

I pushed Keysha down, to get to him, the second she bent over to pick him up.

"What the hell?" We were all igloo, pussy cat frozen.

I dropped to my knees, moving back the ground with my hands, fast! I was beating the dirt with my palms! I was on my knees, pushing the red dirt back and forth. Everyone's eyes were huge, hungry, and anticipating.

Good God, got glad!

"Jackpot!" Dogman shouted.

I laughed and cried at the same damn time!

"Pull it out before I do!" Keysha said, trying to beat me to it.

"Move, child," mom told her.

I regained my composure, then uncovered the safe. "I can't, can't pick it up. Get it Dogman."

"Damn!" Keysha yelled.

"What?"

"It's two of them!"

Everybody froze again. We had all walked off, and Keysha spotted another safe. She should have kept that to herself. Lewis grabbed it.

"Bring it on," I told him.

"What?" he yelled.

"Huh?" I was confused.

Wham! He dropped the second safe, and pulled out a gun.

"This safe comes with me," he said in a serious, dry tone.

He picked up the safe, and walked to the—POW!

"Nigga, please! Give me my money," Kenya said, shooting him in the neck with her pink .380.

"That's my girl," I said, laughing, stepping over the bloody, big-eyed fool.

"Where's my cut?" Keysha asked, looking right at me.

"Here." I tossed her a hundred racks.

"Cool. Hair and nails done for life!" my twin yelled, standing up shaking the money.

We all laughed, however my laugh was hella hard! I had fifteen million dollars!

LIKE A FOOL

Like a fool, the next day, I drove to work, fifteen million bucks richer! I got out of my car, and pimp walked inside the prison.

"Lt., they need to see you in the warden's office," Lt. smart mouth, Joiner said, giving me that 'I told you' stare.

I ignored her, and kept cat walking in my tight, blue uniform like a Top Model for Tyra Banks!

"What up, Joe? You alright?" Shoe-be-do asked.

Shoe-be-do was the orderly who cleaned up on the medical floor. His real name was Josh. He was Blood too, and he looked out for Joe, giving him extra food. Joe was paralyzed, after the last beating he received.

"What's up, Doc?" I asked Doctor Holloway.

"Well, he is paralyzed from the neck down."

"Cool. For how long?" I asked.

She paused . . .

"Forever," she said, and walked away.

Whap!

I smacked him again with the large, hard flashlight. Finally, I saw a tear trying to sneak out of his right eye.

"Inmate! What are you staring at?! You're fired! You damn do boy!" I yelled at the Shoe-be-do clown.

"Damn, Lieutenant. It's like that?" Shoe-be-do asked.

"Yeah, inmate, nigga! Go get another job, and slave for free. I'm rich. Get your weight up, young nigga. Ha, ha." I laughed at him, and walked away.

"Damn, she mean, with a fat donk!" Shoe-be-do said.

"She gone?" Joe asked in a sort of weak tone.

"Yea, bro. Ima look out for you, though. Miss Brown is crazy, man. You need anything before I go, bro? Hold up. Matter of fact, make another phone call," Shoe-be-do said, snatching the cellphone out of his pocket.

"What's the number?!"

"404-..."

"Gotcha," he said, and held the phone to Joe's ear.

"Baby, I love you."

"Love you too."

"What they say?" she asked, anticipating the good news.

"They talking crazy."

"What?! Joe! Tell me what they said!" she ordered.

"They talkin' bout, I'm paralyzed for life," Joe revealed.

Ding!

Daja dropped the phone and cried.

"Get the phone, bro, Ill holla at ya." Joe told the only friend he had left. No other inmate did anything for Joe Brown. He was labeled a snitch, and they thought snitches deserved to die. Snitches get stiches. Even the nurses treated him bad. Shoe-be-do, however, was the prison clown, and high-ranked Pimp City Blood. He didn't believe Joe was a snitch. In his eyes, everyone took Lt. Brown's word, cause she was so damn fine! So, Shoe-be-do stayed loyal to his new friend. They saw each other on the street. Shoe-be-do had been down seven years, and Joe had been down five years.

Twah!

I spit in his face.

"Lieutenant, you can't do that!" nurse Jamie said.

I ran up in her face, like a running back for the Atlanta Falcons!

"And whose gonna stop me?"

Twah!

I spit in her face, and walked to the warden's office. I spit on the nurse and the patient at the same dang time. I said to myself, while walking, dancing, and rapping.

"Ha, ha," I laughed, entering my 'get fired' meeting in the warden's office.

Whoa! I was shocked. Nurse Leslie was there with ten staples in her head!

"That's Miss Brown-," he cleared his throat.

"Excuse me. That's Lt. Brown," I said with an attitude.

"Lt. This is FBI agent Jackson, Miss Sheppard, and Mr. Harper, from Internal Affairs," Deputy Warden Pope said.

Chief counselor Boyd was quiet, and staring dead through my soul. Joe was her nephew, and she was fire hot, pitty pat, pissed. I was as nervous as a chicken on Thanksgiving, in Alabama!

"Nurse Leslie here, has a video of what appears to be you ordering a hit on your children's father, and he shouldn't even be allowed to be on the premises of this prison. Warden Ford, we feel that you must be suspended without pay until further notice-," he paused, and let his fierce words settle on Porsche. She started fidgeting and rolling her eyes.

"Miss Pope, Officer Pope. It appears that you also participated, assisting your best friend, Erica Brown, in revenging her children's father. You failed to follow the proper procedures to notify authorities on your radio," he paused to let it boil on Ashley's soul, like grits. Then everyone's turned to me.

"Now, Lt. Brown, excuse me, back to you, officer Pope. Your assistance will no longer be needed at this prison. You are terminated, without pay. Now, Miss Lt. Erica Brown, we understand,—"

I cut him off, and stood up.

"Naw, yall don't understand a damn thing," then I paused, walking around the room.

"First of fucking all, I don't give a damn about you, this prison, the uniform, the job, the GBI, SSI, or the got damn FBI! Where the hell were yall smart-mouthed, protecting mother fuckers when he broke my nose?! Huh? Where were you when he shot me in public?! Where were you when he raped my damn sister, my best friend, and attempted to rape Officer Pope?! Huh?!

Where were you when he kidnapped me and starved me when I was pregnant with his damn baby?! Where in the collard green hell was you when he broke my damn arm, shot me in the leg, and sent his goons to jump on me at church? Exactly! No fucking where to be found! So yall don't understand a muther fucking thang! I've been a single, black, mother raising two damn kids for five years, by my damn self! Where were you then, Internal Affairs people?! You ain't gave a slut a government dime! Yall giving black men twenty years for hustling, tryna feed his family, yet you give a damn child molester two years! That's why ain't no black men free now!"

"Now, I'm telling all yall Uncle Tom, mutha fuckers. Yall can take me to jail or hell, but you don't have to fire me. Muther fucker! Naw! Yall ain't gotta fire Erica Brown, 'cause Erica Brown quit! Take this cheap paying, house nigga, crooked, correctional officer uniform, and stick it up your law layin' asses!"

Bam! Bam! Whoosh!

I snatched the shirt over my head, and slung it at the FBI agent, knocking the phone on the floor. I kicked off my big black boots, sending them flying across the room, hitting the wall. I had on some skin tight, white, boy shorts, and a white Victoria Secret sports bra. My breast tattoo was exposed, as well as the tattoos on the back of my neck, and the tiger prints that raced up my left leg, to my love spot. I had ten cherries tatted across my pretty, flat stomach. I looked at all the tongues hanging out. I looked at the lusting, perverts, and bisexuals, and stomped right out of the prison!

I jumped into my brand new, 2016, flying, platinum on platinum, fancy Ferrari! I was feeling like a gangsta b. I turned on my Yo Gotti, and blasted out of the prison! I could hear all the male officers and inmates hollering and shouting at my voluptuous, delicious, fine, banging, stripper body!

Yeah! Counting money baby! I had about one-hundred thousand dollars' worth of hundreds scattered all over the front and back floor. I was driving barefoot, but not pregnant!

"Boop!"

I looked down at my pretty, pedicured, red toe nails. Ha, ha, there was a new, crispy, hundred dollar bill under my right foot, on the platinum gas pedal!

Oh well, I just kept my hands on my custom made, platinum steering wheel, that had 'Erica Brown' engraved on it, in diamonds!

IT'S ON

"Mr. Joe Brown, nurse Leslie here, saved the day. She wisely sent the video of your brutal beating, so do you want to sue the state, or work a plea bargain with—"

Joe quickly cut him off.

"Go home. That's what I want. I just want my freedom. Nothing is going right in this stupid chain gang. Let me go. Keep the money!" Joe said, moving nothing but his eyes and mouth.

"What?! But—" Miss Leslie's eyes were as big as the bridge in Jersey. She was devastated. Her pride was crushed like a nut!

"Give her the money. I don't need it."

"Well Mr. Brown, we will give a check to whomever's care you are in. Approximately, one thousand dollars a month, to support you.

Joe was pissed, ashamed, and hated the reality of his circumstances. He knew he still had millions stashed in Joyce Brown's back yard.

Joe had crept into her backyard, at three AM one morning, and buried three safes. Two full of money, and one safe that had real diamonds in it. So, paralyzed or not, he was ready to go!

Bam!

"Bull!" Leslie threw her phone down, and stormed out of the room, pissed. She wanted money, not this crippled, handicapped idiot's freedom. She could give a cold grits in Illinois hell about Joe! She wanted that damn money!

"Any address?" Mr. Reece from Internal Affairs asked.

"Yeah, my sister."

"Your sister? Where does she live?" Amanda asked.

"Seattle."

"No sir. Wrong answer. You must give a Georgia address and make it quick," Amanda said, looking extremely impatient.

"Here, what's the number?" Mr. Reece asked, preparing to dial the number.

Joe called out Daja's number. Mary J's, 'Hood Love,' played and played. Joe was getting absolutely no hood love!

"Daja, come here," Mr. Pimp City said.

She looked up at her tall friend, and shyly blushed. "What, Pimp?"

Pimp City kissed her. She kissed him back, like there was no tomorrow. He picked her up. Bang, slamming her into the wall, still holding her up with his strong, tatted up arms. They kissed like long lost lovers. Like a man fresh out of prison.

Tear! Rip! Rip!

Pimp ripped her lace shirt off, like this was his last chance to have sex. He shoved his mouth on her hard nipples. Her eyes rolled back into her head, and she melted like butter on hot toast. He laid her down on the red carpet, then turned her onto her stomach, and went in.

Smack! Smack!

Pimp was spanking her butt, and pulling her hair. She was soaked. He was long and strong. He banged, pounded it, and beat it for forty minutes straight-Doggy style! Then she got on top. He squeezed her butt, and her nipples as she clawed his tight chest, and rode him fast and hard. He worked his finger inside her juicy, soft butt as she rode him. They both exploded, then she jumped on his face and rode again. He tasted her juices.

Pow! Pow!

"Aww, hell naw!" Kenya PimpCity Brown yelled.

They both froze. The air turned still. The wind stopped blowing. Their sex drive vanished, and they transformed from horny, to horrified.

Kenya aimed the gun at Daja's head, while Daja was still sitting on Pimp's face. Then she aimed at Pimp's private parts and fired.

Pow!

Kenya walked out the room pissed, but not pissed. Who can you trust? Hell, she didn't even trust herself at times.

"Pimp? Pimp? You ok?" Daja asked.

"Ummm, yeah. I'm good, thought she shot my wood," he laughed, finally breathing again.

"She missed?" Daja asked shocked.

"Yeah, on purpose. You know Kenya PimpCity Brown never misses," Pimp laughed.

"You smooth as silk, yourself. Like, how did you survive that bomb?"

"Easy. I was never inside the tank, I had a remote control!" Pimp started laughing.

"Wow," Daja said.

"That's it. I'm getting a girlfriend!" Kenya said, swerving and smoking on the new Keysha, called Kenya-that smoking, fire, African weed!

"Ridin' round smoking on Kenya!" Kenya PimpCity Brown sang loud and laughed.

"Damn a nigga. I'm a fine, sexy, bad, boss chick!"

"Hell naw! You caught them?" I asked Kenya, giggling under my breath. Oh well. Daja and Pimp paid her back I guess. What Goes Around, Comes Around. She had my man so, oh well! LOL.

Pow!

"What the?" Kenya shot at me!

"Trick, I know exactly what you're thinking," Kenya said. She blew a damn hole in the Maserati roof, as we sat in the car, sipping goose.

"Trick, you crazy!" I told Kenya.

"I know, right? That's why I got this . . . Bam!" Kenya yelled.

Even I was as surprised as an alligator, on dry land, in downtown New York!

A short slim, banging, petite, girl with a brown sugar complexion, wavy Barbie doll hair walked up to the car. She was wearing a see through, sexy, lace, black shirt, with a red bra, dark denim skinny jeans that fitted extra right, and some cute black heels. She had on some sweet smelling Burberry perfume. I was amazed.

"Come to momma," Kenya PimpCity Brown said.

She bent over, and kissed Kenya on her lips. She was wearing some sassy, clear lip gloss.

"Trick, where my money?" Kenya snapped.

"Oh, Black didn't give me nothing!" she confessed, looking ashamed.

Kenya PimpCity Brown took a deep puff on the Kush, looked at me, and then back at the cutie.

"Really? So you did it for free?" she asked, smiling.

"Mmmhmm-,"

Ko Boom! Splat!

Kenya PimpCity Brown blew her head completely off, with her red shot gun. Then, a girl who looked exactly like the dead one walked up.

"Identical twins, all in sin, my friend,. Do you have the ends?" Kenya asked.

"Yeah, I got it," the twin said, and gave Kenya a lump of cash.

"Give momma a kiss, good girl," Kenya said, then they sealed the sexy kiss of death.

"Twenty racks," the girl replied.

"Supa kool. Ima talk to my bestie, and get back witcha. See what else you can make before 3 PM," Kenya told her.

"Ok," the cutie said, walking away with that extra twist, making them skinny jeans purr and meow, like a cat!

UH, OH

"Mr. Brown, we just received a teletype from Governor Pope herself. You have an immediate release. Miss Daja is not answering the phone. Do you have any one else who can pick you up?" Miss Joiner asked.

"Damn, I guess. Try. 404- . . . ."

The Nikki Minaj ringtone came on, then it changed to Gucci Mane, 'Making Love to My Money.'

"Hello? Who in the?"

"Miss Brown, Joe Brown has been granted an immediate release, can you come now, to pick him up?"

"Hell n—. Yeah, sure, I'm on my way!" I quickly responded with joy. At first, I was not having it. I was about to curse that lady's wig right off of her head. However, I had a great idea. I did a U-turn in my platinum on platinum Ferrari, in the middle of the busy Tara Blvd.

"Wait, hold up. Please let me roll up," was blasting from my speakers. Man, I felt like a zillion bucks, shawty! (In my real ATL Shawty voice. LOL).

I got to the prison in fifteen, butt naked, stripper seconds! I felt sweeter than an ooey gooey butter cake, in Saint Louis, baby!

I had on my very expensive, eight thousand dollar, red carpet, cream and platinum trimmed Vera Wang dress. I was killing 'em in my fifteen thousand dollar, black Vera Wang heels, baby! My nails had the French, cream tips on them. I smelled like the pretty princess, that I was, wearing my tasty smelling, five hundred dollar, Burberry perfume.

My hair was brand new fresh, thanks to the three hundred dollar African micro braids that went in!

I got out of the car, like, 'yeah, yeah, yeah', and walked through the stupid, prison doors. God, this was slavery to the fullest. Cigarettes were not legal, and went for a hundred dollars a pack. The inmates only ate two times a day; five in the morning, and five at night!

"Hey, Lt. Brown, looking delicious, girl," Officer Jackson said.

I looked at him like, 'whatever, get your weight up, Tom!'

I swallowed when I saw that dirty, once so sexy, super sucker in that wheelchair. He looked like a crippled idiot. Helpless as a worm on the hook.

"Take care of him, Erica," Lt. Joiner said.

"Sure. This is my child's father, trick. Why wouldn't I?" I asked the smart mouth.

"Why wouldn't I?" she mocked me, laughing.

"Whatever, come on dear," I said, all smiles.

He looked calm and cool, but a fool. I pushed him to my Ferrari.

"Whoa! This is fye!" he said, complimenting my ride.

"Thanks, boo." I smiled.

"Yea. Platinum on platinum. Tight to death!" he replied.

Woosh! Whup! Bimp!

"Ouch! Ahhh! You trick!" Joe cried.

"Shut up, Negro!" I steamed, dumping that nigga in the front seat like old trash, and kicking him up the ass with my heels. I looked back at the pitiful prison job, and shot them the bird, twice!

Then, I turned on the throwback Tupac. 'Ima straight rider, you can't deny it, you don't wanna f . . . wit me . . .'

Whap!

I back slapped him, and kept dancing to my gangsta partner, Pac! Joe was folded awkward, his head was stuck in the passenger floor, legs as stiff as stone, with his butt in the air, but I didn't really give a hot bacon damn!

Then, I drove him to my new, secret house in the slap dark middle of nowhere! Wilmington, North Carolina! No one would hear a word. The town didn't even have street lights, and the next house was a mile away!

I pulled up in the long, dark driveway.

"Ok, trick! I'm home! Welcome to the Wrath of Erica, Beat down, Brown!" I laughed, like the wicked witch of Wilmington.

Whack!

I opened the car door, and snatched him out of the car, by his neck, with two hands!

Rffffff.

I drug him by his legs through the rocky driveway, and up the four wooden steps, through the living room.

Kick! Wooh! Boom! Boom! Bang! Zang!

I opened the door, by ramming it open with his head. Then, I karate kicked him down the steps, upside-down, he rumbled down like a cracked egg!

"Mommy, what is dat?" my son asked.

"A RAT!" I lied, truthfully.

"Ooooh, Mommy! That's a big 'ole rat!" 3Pac yelled, while jumping up and down.

"Baby, you got him?" Shoe-be-do whispered in my ear.

"Yeah baby, I got him. Give me a kiss."

Muwah.

We kissed. Shoe-be-do also got out earlier that morning. After the 8 AM prison count. I was in the parking lot of the prison, with a short, North Carolina jersey on, and no shoes or panties. That nigga banged me thirty minutes long, and hard. Then ate me all the way from GA to North Carolina!

I was four months pregnant by Shoe-be-do, and we got married, at the court house that morning. I had been having sex with him at the nurses' station of the prison. I made sure he took care of Joe, so I could punish him! I set the entire set up into play, by telling Shoe-be-do to give Nurse Leslie the phone idea. I walked into the prison with the phone up my cat! Yeah. Tight fit, but it snapped right back to tight size. I got that snap back! Lol.

I knew Leslie would take the bait. The entire set-up was my plan. I wanted him to get an early release, so I could kick the skin color off his ass! I knew they couldn't fire me. Hell, I didn't transfer him there, Atlanta did! I just worked there. So what?!

"Mommy, I'm hungry, can you get the Fruit Loops from up there, mommy?" Crymeka asked, looking like a six year old, Halle Berry. So innocent, light, and cute.

"Yeah, baby." I reached on top of the fridge, and poured the cereal.

Crymeka was wearing her red Minnie Mouse shirt. She just smiled, and ate the cereal.

"Bam!" 3Pac yelled! He was in an uproar over the Atlanta Falcons throwing the game's winning touchdown over their rivals, the New Orleans Saints. My son was unbeatable in the football game.

"PlayStation fifteen, baby!" 3 Pac yelled. "3 Pac back! 3 Pac back! That's what all theses suckas yelling man, 3 Pac back!" he rapped his five year old, self-made remix. He was always rapping.

JACKPOT!

"Yeaaah! Makin' Love to the money!" Keysha sang, walking from car to car.

"So what you like?" the short, Mexican-looking white guy named Dustin asked.

"Yeah, how much is it?" Keysha asked, grippin' her McDonald's book bag.

"Well this Porsche is fully loaded and equipped with turbo boost, my new upgrade. Special addition. It-."

"Sir, how much is it?" she asked the salesman.

"Well, this baby goes for one-hundred and seventy thousand. We also have another Porsche, a little cheaper, but it-."

"No! I want it. Here." Keysha gave him two hundred thousand dollars. He looked baffled, confused, and lost like a white deer in the jungle, staring at a lion.

"Ummm. Well, actually, this is wonderful. But two-hundred thousand is too much to spend at one time. So, what I'll do to be safe, so the FEDs and IRS won't be on us, I'll write it off as payment in the computer, but-,"

"Keys." Keysha said, totally ignoring him. He looked goofy and cute to her at the same dang time. He fumbled, then looked up and down, and all around.

"Oh, ha, ha, silly me. They're in my hand. Here," he said, handing her the keys to her new, red Porsche, trimmed in gold.

"Hey Dustin, you're a cutie. Call me," she said, writing her number on a hundred dollar bill, then speeding out of the car lot, smiling.

He just stood there, like it was a dream!

"Awww! Luck has finally changed for me! Thank God! Ha, ha, and what a coincidence. I turn on the radio, and Keysha Cole is on!" Keysha laughed.

That day, in her mom's backyard, when Keysha kept digging, and found the other safe filled with money, she found something else.

Keysha found a bag of real diamonds that originally came straight from a king in Kenya, Africa!

King Levi!

She only kept one diamond, and sold the other ten for one billion dollars to an oil owner, named Sook, in the Middle East. She met him on Facebook.

No one knew! However, after all the pain and let-downs that Keysha had, she had finally been rewarded. Keysha is the most popular, black female name ever used in American history. Originally an African name that people rapped about, Keysha had finally made it bigger than anybody she knew!

TWINS

"Twins, shut up!" Kenya PimpCity Brown yelled to her twins, Coca-Cola Brown and Cocaine Brown.

"But mommy, I want the red snow boots, not the pink! Pink is for punks!" Cola wined.

"Shut it, Cola. That's not nice."

"And I want the all-white Forces, not the red and black J's (Jordans)," Cocaine added.

"All right, all right, all ready. Yall got too many demands for four year olds. Here," Kenya said, giving them their own damn money.

"Girl, Nu Nu and Lexie ain't no betta. Super spoiled!" Porsche said, laughing, while sucking on her strawberry milk shake, through her red straw.

"Naw, mama. I just want my own money to shop," Lexie confessed.

"Here." Porsche said, sticking ten balled-up hundred dollar bills in her hand.

"Next? Nails, toes, hair, and clothes," Nu Nu said, with one hand on her hip, and her right hand stuck out for the money, wiggling her fingers.

"Here Nu Nu," Porsche said, handing Nu Nu a thousand new dollars, with the swagg and ease of a rich author's wife!

"Hello? Keysha?" Lexie asked, on her iPhone.

"Naw, shawty. It's Keysha TooRich Brown! New Year. New Money. New Fame, and a new name! WOOOH! In my Nature Boy Rick Flair voice!" Keysha said, laughing out loud, while lying on a silver beach towel, in the Bahamas, on the beach.

"Well, excuse me, honey with the brand new money. Let me let you talk to mommy," Lexie joked in her rap voice, giving Porsche the purple phone.

"Guuuuurl, I heard about you and Miss PimpCity Brown," Keysha TooRich Brown said, as she got a back massage on the beach, by a pretty white girl, and a muscle man at the same dang time!

"Noooo! Girl, what you heard?" Porsche asked sarcastically.

"Trick, I heard you and Kenya found two more big ass diamonds in the back yard that day," Keysha said, laughing.

"Truuuuuue!" Porsche bragged.

"But actually, Lexie and Cocaine found it, keepin' it trill," Kenya chipped in, with a grin.

BAM!

"Wrong answer, buddy," Lexie said, kicking the dude in the chest at Foot Locker.

His huge, three-inch thick glasses flew off of his face! Lexie kicked him so hard, he flew backwards into the Nike shoe rack, and knocked fifty shoes on the floor!

"Whoa. Hard kick for a fourteen year old," Kenya said, laughing.

"Reminds me of the young me," Porsche added, while laughing.

Kick! Slap! Then, a Nike Flip Flap, by Nu-Nu.

"Don't ever bump into the Brown girls. We don't play in GA!" Nu Nu said.

All the girls laughed, and gave each other high-fives, then continued to shop.

"Yall crazy. I shoulda stuck a ounce of cocaine in his mouth for touching my cousin!" Cocaine yelled like the brown-skinned, four year old Hulk!

"No, no, bro. Let it go," Cola said, holding back her twin brother.

"Let's ride," Kenya PimpCity Brown said to the crew.

"What's yo name, Lil Mama?" a slim, Augusta gangsta, named Tee-Tee asked.

She froze in a pose. She stared at him from head to toe, in his all-white everything.

"Porsche Mercedes Beauty Ford Brown," Porsche said, with her hands on her slim waist, booty round, and poking out of those stretch pants, like BOO YAH!

"All dat, huh? Well here's my number. Hit me up, sexy," Tee-Tee said.

He wrote his number on a three hundred dollar bill with Obama's face on it! Then he walked away with Lisa, his swagged out, rich, Queen Pen mom. Augusta GA's finest.

"Damn. Where dey do dat at?" Porsche said, holding the Obama, black President, three-hundred dollar bill up, to see if it was really real! What in the BOOP?!

HOT DOG

"Hot Dog!"

Whap!

"Ha, ha, Shoe-be-do, you crazy!" I laughed at Shoe-be-do for smacking Joe with a raw piece of pork chop and ten raw hot dogs.

Whamp!

I smacked him with a raw, live fish!

"Take that, tuff guy!" Shoe-be-do said, smacking him in the eye with an onion.

Whack!

"Food fight! Food fight!" I yelled like a hyped up, high school teenager on food fight Friday!

Whap! Bam! Bap!

Me and Shoe-be-do both hit him all over his face and body, with food we had in a basket. We had so much fun, racing to see who could smack him first. We hit the bad guy with hot bake potatoes, raw lettuce, pears, watermelons, plums, packs of Now-And Laters, grapes, Cokes . . .

"Take that, Joe Brown!"

Booh yah!

I cracked his knee with his old, high school baseball bat, immediately knocking it out the socket.

"Boop!" I said, laughing.

"Shoe-be-do!" Shoe-be said, in his cartoon voice, laughing.

Zzzzzzrrrrr.

We both dragged him into another room.

I only fed him bread and water.

"Umph!"

I stuffed his mouth full of balled-up white bread.

"Poof!"

I punched the bread down his throat while he was trying to chew.

Whap!

"Bad boy!" Shoe-be-do said, smacking him in the head with a loaf of bread.

Splash.

"Swallow, sucker!" I said, as he choked, coughed, and gagged for air.

I tossed a whole pitcher of ice water in his face, up his nose, and in his eyes. His eyes were blood shot red, like he had pink eye. He stuck his tongue out, fighting to lick the drips of water off his lips.

Bam! Snap!

I kicked him in the head, breaking my heels.

"You remember your best friend in prison that took care of you? Now he taking care of your once faithful, pretty, fine, baby momma. AND he is taking care of YOUR two kids that you are too lame to hold. Ha, ha. Mr. So Hard, Tough, Joe Brown, laying on the ground with blood, eggs, and food all over your damn, ugly face! I just broke your damn leg!"

Pow!

I shot him in the other leg.

"AND I just shot you. Now, What Goes Around Comes Back Around, Joe Brown!" I yelled, walking in circles, expressing myself, because he never had time to listen.

"You slept with my best friend, behind my back. You tried to rape Ashley, not even knowing who she was, because she had on a wig, and had green contacts in her eyes. You raped Kenya PimpCity Brown, and Keysha who's now a billionaire, 'cause she just called me from Jamaica saying she got a billion dollars for your bag of diamonds. I only get fifteen million, but it can't compare to the zillion dollar hurt, pain, and shame you gave me. I woulda gave all this money back and this new baby I'm pregnant with, by your friend. I would give it all back, Joe. Just to be the only woman you ever slept with. Like you were the only man I ever slept with."

"Joe, I tried to change my life. You had me getting beat up. At church! You had some crack head pull out a gun on our new born baby! You gave me a disease while I was pregnant! You beat me, and made me miscarry our first child, who woulda been eight years old! And since you slept with my friends behind my back, I'm sleeping with yours in your face!"

"You tied me up, kidnapped me, and made me watch you have sex with strippers. Now, I'm kidnapping you, and I'm about to go straight upstairs and have sex in the room right over your head, so you can hear. AND, Ima let you watch the video, of us making love in prison, on your bed! I gave him head, on your bed! Hey, that rhyme, Joe Brown. Man, I hate you, dog!"

"I hate that you made me hate you," I said, crying in Shoe-be-do's arms.

I didn't want to hate anybody. I didn't want to be this cruel. God knows I felt bad. But I wanted this nigga to hurt like I hurt, so it is what it is!

"Damn you, Joe! Shoe-be-do, let's go." I pushed play, and the surround sounds in the basement came on. There was a speaker in every corner.

The T.V.'s showed me and his friend on nine T.V.'s, making love in prison, in the house, and in the same basement he was in.

Then, I bent over in Joe's face.

"Give it to me, daddy. Hit it like Joe's paralyzed ass wish he could! But he ain't as big as you, Shoe-be-do! Make it do what it do!" I said, in a nasty, naughty, freaky voice.

Shoe-be-do hit me doggy style, right in his face.

"Ahhh! Daddy! Daddy! Joe's best friend! Oh, you better! You better! You the best! Shoe-be! Shoe-be! Shoe-be-do! Shoe-be-do! I, I, I, love you!"

He humped me fast and hard.

Joe lay there helpless, crying like a punk, while his homeboy beat it up! I was on a movie screen T.V. on the ceiling above him, and in every corner, having sex on all 80 inches on the flat screen T.V. It was super loud on the twenty-two inch speakers! It sounded like a sex concert, with a hundred people having sex at the same dang time!

I was bent over, touching the floor. After Shoe-be-do got weak in me, he got on his knees and licked me from the back, while I was bending over.

Ooohhh. This felt so good!

"Let's go finish," he said, picking me up, and carrying me upstairs.

"Hold up! Joe! Got something for you boo! You know I can't do you like that! Sick him, boy!" I yelled.

The pit bull sprinted down the stairs like a track star!

"Roof! Roof! Roof!"

"Ahhh! Ahhh! Enough! Enough! Get him off me! Erica! Erica! I'm sorry! Please! Get this dog! Ahh! Ahh! Help! Shoe-be-do!" Joe begged, pleaded, and bled!

Poof!

I closed the door, ignored him and the dog, and made love, right above his head.

'Dive in,' played on the surround sound in the room. My slim, fine, brown, prison-tatted, hardcore man, dove in! Deep!

"Roof! Roof"! The dog . . .

Smack! Smack! My man . . .

Ahhh! Ahh!"" Joe . . .

Dive in. Trey . . .

I knew the dog was having a ball! Probably eating that fool alive! Ha, ha, with all that food that we left on that idiot!

Lucky for Joe, the dog got tired of chewing on him, and ate the raw meat we left downstairs. The dog fell asleep. The porn video of his best friend, and former baby, ended. Me and Shoe-be-do fell asleep, sweating. He held me from the side and kissed my neck, still inside of me, until we fell into dream world.

EASTER SUNDAY

"Erica. Erica Brown," a deep voice said. I struggled to get up, yawned, and looked at the clock on the T.V. that read 3 AM.

"Who dat?" I froze. A man was standing in my bedroom, wearing all white. He had on a white 'A' hat (a for angel, not Atlanta), a white t-shirt, white jeans, and white tennis shoes.

"That's enough punishment on him. Revenge belongs to God. Anything else you do, will come back worse on you. Repent or Burn. Forgive or die. God loves you, Erica Brown."

Flash!

The man vanished.

"Shoe-be! Baby! Did you hear him?" I hit him on the shoulder.

"Huh?!" He popped up, stared at me, and went slap, back to sleep. I had to laugh at my baby. However, I got up, and prayed. I couldn't sleep. I read the book of James.

I took a good bath, and put on my five-thousand dollar, Versace, Easter dress. Shoe-be-do put on his five-thousand dollar, Louis Vuitton suit. We got the kids dressed. Crymeka had beautiful, African, micro braids, and wore a red, pretty dress. 3Pac, with his tough and handsome self, had on an all-white suit, with a black shirt and shoes.

I went downstairs, and fed Joe some Frosted Flakes! But . . .

Whap! One last slap!

We rode to church in the back of our limo, all the way to the ATL. Green was our driver. He was cool and calm.

I asked for forgiveness. It was time to be a woman, a mother, and a wife.

Shoe-be knew the word of God, and he also wanted a change. We pulled up in the large, beautiful parking lot of the Ray of Hope International Ministry, in Decatur, GA. The awesome Evangelist Hannah Sheppard, and Pastor Joshua Levi Brown, Assistant Pastor Lisa Daniels, and Choir Director, Lavonda Williams were the leaders of the church.

"Praise God!" Aunty Glory Ann said. She was with my gorgeous cousin, Shay.

Shay was dark and lovely with long, pretty hair.

"Hey girl! I miss you," I told Shay, hugging her.

"Erica!" I heard, and turned around to see my other preaching cousin.

"Well, well," Butterball said.

"Hey Trica!" I said to my beautiful, young cousin.

Everyone was there for Easter.

"Pookie! Aaliyah!" I shouted, hugging them.

Porsche and Kenya walked up and hugged me.

"So what's been up?" Devin said, in her pretty, purple dress.

"Nothin', girl."

"Wooosh!" we all said, when Keysha pulled up in a pink Rolls Royce, bumping gospel music.

Me and Keysha hugged. "I love you, girl."

"What about momma?!" my mom said, sneaking up behind me with Bre'Shauna and Uncle Chi.

"What up, Erica?" Daja said, holding Champ's hand.

"Love you." I said, hugging Daja.

Uncle O.G. Hood and Dog Man both had on all-white tuxedos. White boy, Scott, had on a fresh, black suit, and winked his eye at me at least fifteen times!

"Saint Louis, baby! South side!" Scott yelled, laughing with his son, West-side.

"Hey, my favorite cousin." Santana said, wearing a money green Polo suit, smelling fresh. He was with Summerhill, Goldy, Dirty, and Black Child. The Mob looked nice. I hugged Santana.

"I love you, cuz," I whispered in his ear.

"Awwwe. Erica, you look beautiful!" Ashley said, walking up in her sexy, yellow, Versace dress.

"Girl, you know you are the best beautician in the world! You did your own hair, again?" I asked her.

"Yeah girl, you know it," she said, smiling like a five year old at my compliment.

Everyone looked perfect. It felt perfect. Easter Sunday. I went to church, and listened to Minister Robin lead the praise team.

"Oh." I jumped when my brother, Dontae kissed me.

I sat next to Miss Millsap, her niece, and her pretty daughter.

Aunty Velma was standing with Jameka and Jasmine, my two Candler Rd. cousins. We waved at each other.

"Please stand for prayer. God, this Easter Sunday we praise you because we are all here and alive to see this day. Many didn't make it. We have lost so many lives. Young and old. Rich and poor. Famous and unknown. Lord, we know that in all things, you make it work for the good, for those that believe. While we're here and alive today, I ask you to forgive us and save us from our sins. Help us all to become what you created us to be. Remove all the negative forces and doubts, away from us. The devil can't win! We can't win, in sin! Jesus, Jesus, is our only friend! Through his stripes we are healed! Amen!" Minister Joshua Levi Brown prayed.

I felt the chills, anoint my body. I felt so blessed.

Then, Evangelist Hannah Sheppard came to the pulpit, wearing a beautiful white dress.

"Hallelujah! Praise him. When the praises go up, the blessings come down. Praise God. Give him the Praise. He is worthy! This beautiful, Easter Sunday! What a powerful prayer from Minister Brown. Open your Bibles to the book of Galatians. For those who don't know, it's in the New Testament, toward the back of the Bible."

"Galatians Chapter 6:7. The title of the sermon is, WHAT GOES AROUND, COMES AROUND."

"It reads in verse seven, Do not be deceived, God cannot be mocked. A man reaps, what he sows. Know that God can't be deceived, tricked, or fooled. You cannot get over on God. God cannot be mocked."

"Now, Apostle Paul wrote the book of Galatians, from prison. He wrote it to the churches in Galatia. Paul was making it clear to you, that

God cannot be mocked. Mock is in the dictionary. It means to make fun of, to laugh at, or to copy what people say or do. God will NOT be made fun of or laughed at."

"Now, a man reaps what he sows. To reap. Reap means to collect, harvest, or to obtain goods as a result of something that you have done. Now, sow, means to plant or spread seeds in or on the ground, or to introduce or spread feelings or ideas, especially ones that cause trouble."

"Now, you REAP WHAT YOU SOW, means you reap or collect whatever you sow or spread in life. You get out of life, what you put out of your life. If you live by the sword, you die by the sword. If you do bad, bad will come back on you. If you do good, good will come back on your life."

"So, I encourage you people to do good! Because the Bible tells you, What Goes Around, Comes Around. Apostle Paul wrote the book, and he used to kill Christians. Now he was suffering in prison, writing the word of God, because he once did wrong to believers. He wrote most of the New Testament from prison. Like Joshua here, wrote most of his International Best Sellers from prison."

"This Easter, and every day after, do good, so good will come back. Amen!" Evangelist Sheppard spoke.

"Hallelujah!" D.J. shouted out of nowhere.

"Boop." Detective Walker said, smiling when I turned around and saw her and my Chinese and black homeboy, J.B., standing behind me.

The entire church stood on their feet, and praised God.

"Love . . . So many people use your name in vein. Love . . ." Bre'Shauna started singing with ATL's superstar, Mizz Tye. Ribbons started falling out of the ceiling.

"God!" I celebrated and cried when I turned around, only to see my mother in a long, beautiful, wedding dress. She was getting married!

I was mad shocked that I didn't know! But I was happy. Plus, he was fine! He had T.I.'s looks, and a heavy weight boxer body! Go mama! Go mama! Go!

Joshua's beautiful, baby girl, Asia, was walking my mom down the aisle. Asia smiled, and waved me.

Destiny and Saniya were in the choir, singing backup for my niece, Bre'Shauna.

Boom!

Even Trapp got saved today! Then, he still had the nerve to throw up the Big B's Blood sign when he gave it all to God—in his all red, fifteen thousand dollar suit!

"Meet me at the alter in your white dress, we ain't getting no younger, we might as well do it, do it!" the best, hottest, new, successful, R&B singer, from East Atlanta, Mizz Tye sang. She brought the house down when she sang! Just like in Columbia High! Mizz Tye was a sexy, chocolate, beautiful, sensational singer!

"Pap! Yeah! Yeah!" Roscoe clapped as loud as a jet and a rocket in my ear. He took his dog gone shirt off in the church! All because Mizz Tye was singing!

Whap!

I smacked Roscoe with a roll of Sherman toilet tissue in the mouth.

"Boy, put your shirt back on, in church!" I laughed.

"Oh, ha, ha. Dang it. Mizz Tye the best singer in the world! I love that girl! Dang! Let me put my clothes back on though. Shookie, dookie, Erica. I thought I was on 106th & Park!" Roscoe joked.

"No! Roscoe, you at the Ray of Hope International Ministries! And Mama Brown getting married. Now if you don't sit your party like a rock star, chicken hawk head, Newport tongue, bird brain, pencil body, karate ear, collard green-chewing, New York, ATL living, loud, hot sauce mouth, butt down!! And put you shirt back on, boy! In the name of the black Jesus!!!" I exclaimed.

"The Jesus with the Afro!!!" Kenya said, laughing and cracking everybody up!

"Oh, my gosh," I said in my white girl voice! Not in my Austell Baby Land voice. Kenya you still crazy ass a monkey in a thong!" our cute cousin, Mz. Dee said, laughing.

"Excuse me, ladies and gentlemen, God is so, so, extremely good. Did yall not hear about Mz. Porsche PrettySwag Brown?" Porsche asked.

"Huh?" we all replied.

"Bah, hah! I married a billionaire from Saudi Arabia yesterday! The prune was ninety years old, he died last night! He left me one billion dollars!" Porsche yelled!

"True!" Kenya PimpCity Brown cheered, walking out of the church with her own fifty thousand dollar, custom made, white, ReKeDe blouse, white matching skirt, and Christian Louis Vuitton boots.

"What you all excited and crunck about?" Mr. Pimp City asked her, in his all black, two-hundred thousand dollar tuxedo.

Kenya PimpCity Brown gave him that 'get the heck out of my face, nigga' look. "My girlfriend just hit big."

"So, I always did it big for you, Kenya. Dang. Took you to every five star restaurant in America. Bought you every pair of shoes you wanted. A new outfit every day. What's the hype about? Women lie, men lie, numbers don't lie. I spent at least a million on you, this year! Nobody's perfect, so what's up? Can we get back together? That girl on girl thang ain't about nothing. You gonna get tired of licking, and need a REAL man on your team to protect you-,"

"Hold up! That's where you wrong! Kenya PimpCity Brown takes care of Kenya PimpCity Brown, Buddy Roe! The only protection I need is from God, and my trigger finger! Plus, I don't need you! I'm a pimp, myself! Plus, even though my bottom chick just committed suicide, she gave me five million before she died. Robbed five banks for me! Now, I'm 'bout to go worldwide with my Kenya PimpCity Brown, custom made, Monstar earrings, and my ReKeDe clothing line!"

"Whoa, you talkin about the earrings that the president's wife, and the Queen had on this morning, promoting?" he asked, as stunned as a giraffe with a short neck.

"Ha, ha. Yep. I just got a deal, nigga. But I love you-no-,"

"Kenya, girl, I love you. I'm sorry. Even though you probably won't' forgive me—"

"Shhhh."

Muwahh.

Kenya put her finger over Daja's mouth, and kissed her on the lips.

"Baby, we coulda humped this nigga together. I don't care about that. What Goes Around, Comes Around. I love you, and Pimp at the same dang time!" Kenya yelled.

They all laughed and hugged each other.

"Awww, ain't that poodle, puppy, pretty?!" Devin said, laughing.

"Oh, I got good news and bad news," Daja said, instantly changing the mood.

"What?" Kenya asked.

"My dad died . . ."

"Awww. I'm sorry," Devin said.

"Bam! Bingo! But, he left me six million, a fifteen bedroom mansion in Seattle and the hospital in Atlanta!" Daja shouted.

"And she secretly had a baby girl. We named her Skinny Smalls," Mr. Pimp City added.

Kenya looked at him and laughed.

"Is this part true, Daja? You hid a pregnancy, and Champ ain't the daddy? What Champ say?" Kenya asked.

Bam!

Out of nowhere, Champ ran up in his green tuxedo, and knocked Mr. Pimp City out!

Splash! Splash!

"Wake up, Pimp!" Mizz Tye said, throwing the glass of water that she had, on his face.

Pow!

Pimp woke up, and shot Champ in his fighting hand.

"Oh, so you think I can't use my left hand?!" Champ said, trying to swing.

Pow!

"Now, box with no hands," Mr. Pimp City said, and walked away with Daja.

Pow!

Champ shot Champ!

"What the?" I was stunned, when I ran up in the last end of the church crime scene. I was scratching my head, and so was Daja, Pimp, Kenya PimpCity Brown, and Dee.

"I'm the real Champ. That was a crack head that I dressed up to look like me. I used him for three of my big plays in Atlanta. Oh well, I can't use him again. But Daja, I just wanted to see who your heart was with. I loved you. Still do. But it's cool. 'Cause God made my last play a hit! The one called, 'Lord, Let My People Go,' just became a movie. Made eight-hundred thousand last weekend. So I'm blessed, and I'm marrying your first cousin, Danika," Champ said, and walked off.

Then he got into the Benz with Danika, bumping Chris Brown, 'Deuces!'

"Big deal. You Daja PimpCity Brown now! You rich! Welcome to the ghetto, pimp rich, Brown family!" Kenya PimpCity Brown said, giving me, Daja, Pimp, Dee, and now Shoe-be a high five.

"What's this? Is he dead?" Reverend Joshua asked, walking up with Evangelist Hannah Sheppard.

We all froze.

"I think," I said in a low, shy voice.

"You think, but I know, Jesus can do ANYTHING. Every time me and Evangelist Sheppard pray, God moves. In Jesus name, get up, and walk!" Joshua spoke.

Wooh!!!

The Champ look-alike got up and left!

Now this was one of the longest, wildest days of my life! However unlike a Final Destination, you can beat What Goes Around, Comes Around, only if you change your life, and do good. Give it to God. I learned that today. 'Cause all in all, we all prayed, and God saved. We all changed our lifestyles, we were all millionaires, but kept God first. We had a lot of fun.

It had been a long day. I fell asleep on the ride back from ATL to North Carolina.

I dozed off, exhausted, buddy! It was twelve midnight, when we got to Wilmington.

King Shoe-be-do picked me up, and carried me into the house.

"Dang!"

"What?" he paused.

"Joe . . . I gotta check on Joe. I got to help him. I've done enough. I don't want God to punish me. Dear God, forgive me for my sins, and the way I've treated Joe Brown. Forgive me for every person I smacked and hurt. In Jesus name I pray, Amen," I prayed.

When I entered the house, I walked downstairs. I covered my nose. It smelled like pregnant, hog dookey, and elephant diarrhea fart! Joe had the funk kicking like karate!

"Joe, I'm sorry. Please forgive me. And I forgive you for everything. I'm tired. I had a surprise wedding today. Mom and Keith got married. Ima bathe you. Here, eat this quarter pounder cheese burger, baby," I said, washing his face, and feeding him.

Shoe-be picked him up and sat him in the chair, until he got done eating Mickey D's hot, famous fries.

"I'll be back in the morning, Joe. I apologize. No more Miss Wrong," I told him, and stumbled up the steps, tired.

Bloop!

Shoe-be caught me.

"I gotcha, boo," he said, and carried me up the steps. I immediately crashed out!

WHO SHOT YAH?

'I'm Different...I'm Different...' blasted from the speakers inside Pimp City Strip Club on Candler Rd.

Santana was high as a fly, getting a lap dance from the yellow, sexy, hot, Columbian diva, Micki. She was bent over, touching the floor with her yellow, manicured nails. She was doing wonders with that juicy, fruity booty. She made each cheek clap together like a standing ovation.

"Dog!" he yelled, when Micki did a head stand.

She stood on her head, and spread her legs wide open. Then she hit a split, proving she was once a gymnast. To top it off, she put her legs behind her head, as she lay on the floor. Then, she smoked a blunt with her cat! San was amazed and shocked as a pink Incredible Hulk with no muscles!

Then, Kelly and Future pumped loud as a college band, from the speakers.

"I don't wanna neva end!!!" Santana shouted, rapping to the old hit song.

Smush...

Micki sat in his lap, running her fingers through her red hair.

"You like that, daddy?" she asked.

He stared at her breasts. They seemed to sing Christmas carols to him.

Slice...

San's eyes hopped open like a public bathroom!

He grabbed his throat. His neck was sliced wide open, like Wal-Mart!

Pow!

The killer shot him in the head. No one heard a sound. The music was deafening loud. The sweet potato muffled the blast from the nickel plated .22 Magnum.

"Hey! You ok?" Cheetara asked Micki.

Micki had her hand over her mouth, shaking in fear. Her hazel eyes were crying. Blood was splattered all over her pretty face and body.

The killer slid through the now screaming, shocked crowd.

Cheetara tightly escorted the horrified, bloody Micki to the bathroom.

"Are yo sure you're ok?" Cheetara asked her nude, red best friend.

Speechless . . .

"Boo!"

Cheetara jumped, then looked behind her.

"Guuurl, don't do that!" Cheetara told Dreauna.

They both laughed and hugged each other.

While their attention wasn't focused on Micki, she made a quick move.

Spiff . . .

She spit the razor in her hand, then swoop . . .

She tossed it down the drain of the sink.

'Did you get away?' Micki texted Santana's killer.

Zzzzmp.

Her phone vibrated.

"Yea," the shooter replied.

Excellent team work. Micki sliced Santana's throat. Then, pow!

The killer shot him.

"Miss Micki, are you ok?" Officer Walker asked the innocent-looking/terrified actress.

Micki looked horrified. Her eyes were puffy and watery.

"It's ok. It's ok," Lt. Jackson assured her.

"Well, let her go. Leave her alone. She witnessed enough for one night," Detective Tiffani Bryson said, as she allowed Micki to leave.

"Hold on! One question—"

Everyone paused in the loud, mixed-perfume smelling, pink-painted, strip club bathroom.

"Who shot yah?" Officer Walker asked.

LAUGH NOW, CRY LATER

Joe stood up, and took a shower. He looked at his Rolex. Four in the morning.

"Cool, I'm Gucci," Joe said, then grabbed Shoe-be-do's golden .38 special.

Joe had been exercising. He could walk again, however, no one knew. He had been walking for an entire month!

He put on his ski mask, another toy he found, while rumbling around when we were gone. Then, he put on his gloves, and dressed in Shoe-be-do's all black outfit. It was time to pay Erica and Shoe-be back. It was over. He had a clean, perfect escape. The advantage of being kidnapped for the past twelve months was that no one knew he was there. He would burn our bodies, and throw them in the Mississippi River.

"Look at them—naked, knocked out on top of the cover. No vest, protection, or weapons. This is my easiest kill ever," Joe whispered to himself.

"Erica first. Shoe-be-do gets done second."

He aimed. Fired.

Pow! Pow! . . . Pow!

Dead quiet. Not a soul spoke. The room seemed and felt scary and spooky, like we were in a horror film.

I couldn't believe my eyes. I looked at Shoe-be, and he looked at me. We sat up in the bed. Then, I stood up, and covered my nude body with a white silk sheet.

I looked at Joe's head. Surely, he was dead this time. How did he get in here? So all this time, he really could walk? Did the nurse and the prison triple cross my double cross, for revenge? He could have killed me!

Now, his brains were splattered all over my bedroom wall.

"Baby, give momma the gun," I told my son.

"But daddy was gonna kill you, Mommy," my son said, while looking so innocent.

I just looked at him, and slowly grabbed the red, painted .380 out of his hand.

My six year old son killed his own father. He was too young to realize what he had done. But, he wasn't too young to cry. However, 3Pac didn't shed one tear or show any remorse. Evidently, he felt like he did no wrong. He felt like protecting his mother's life was right.

3Pac was the only one who knew Joe could walk. He would sneak downstairs, feed Joe, and play with him. Maybe 3Pac knew the plan, or sensed it. Pac is never woke at four AM. Maybe it was the ghost of the baby we lost, that woke 3Pac up, crying for revenge on his evil daddy.

Rachael and the Channel 5 news was at my house at 7:00 AM.

FBI Agent Walker had moved up in rank, and assured me she would resolve the entire incident, and that no punishment would come to my son. Hell, he was only 6 . . .

The next day, at school, 3Pac was on the playground, having fun. He was pushing his beautiful, little girlfriend, LaVodka, on the swing.

Woooosh!

She went soaring through the air, like a bald eagle.

Ka Boom!

LaVodka hit the ground, hard, breaking her arms and legs.

"Get up, you little trick!" 3Pac said.

Then he drug the girl by her legs, which were bent backward. He drug her leg first, head last, up the sliding board, then . . .

Wooom! Boom!

He pushed her back down the sliding board! The beautiful, mixed girl, crashed on the dirt. Hard!

3Pac then slid down the slide, like a skateboarder, picked the already injured girl up, and power slammed her!

Boom!

-In the middle of the playground!!!!

Like father, like son! Was 3Pac the next Joe Brown?!

I pray not ...

To be continued ...

LOVE DON'T HATE

You say you love me,
but you treat me wrong.
You cheated and had sex with another girl in our home.
You say you love me,
But I can't tell.
You turned your back on me, when I went to jail.
You say you love me,
But you hit on me.
You blacked my eye, to the point that I can't see.
You say you love me, but you put your friends first.
When I'm down, you make me feel worse.
You say you love me,
But when I needed a ride,
You found out we couldn't have sex, so you ran to hide!
You say you love me,
But you let me fight over you!
You're never faithful, loyal, or true!
You say you love me,
But you show so much hate,
There is no debate, LOVE DON'T HATE!

SHOUT OUT TO MY REAL . . .

I lost my father, but I found my sister and brothers.

Cimeon, Sergio, Shawn and Deon, now we finally met each other.

30 plus years, I wondered where my dad's kids were at.

Now I know yall blessed, and balling like that.

I love yall and see yall soon.

In Real Life, Real Talk, no goofy cartoon.

Erica Bailey, what a special person you are.

Writing this book, I couldn't see this far.

However, you have five kids, and work two jobs every day!

Never met me, but typed my books for me, anyway!

Don't ever, ever, get any realer than that!

Thank you, Erica. You got my back.

Shout out to Micki Pettis, who rode two busses and a train.

Three hours to TBN T.V. station, to get my book from my mom, with no shame!

Shout out to Liz, once again.

Buying so many copies of my book, that's a super friend!

Shout out to Danika Holloway, for buying my books
   and spreading them all across the world.
Friendship is more precious than gold, diamonds and
   pearls.
Love you, mom, and thank you for seeing my dreams!
God, thank you for keeping me alive, to accomplish
   things!

SHORT STORY- VAMPIRES IN THE STRIP CLUB
BY JOSHUA LEVI BROWN

CHAPTER I
DROP IT LIKE IT'S HOT

'I'm in Love With a Stripper' blasted from China's yellow Benz.

"Money Monday! Them niggas makin' it rain up in that thang tonight!" China Doll told Kenya.

"Guuuurl, you ain't neva lied!" Kenya said, chilling in all pink, while smokin' on a blunt of Kenya.

"Ima make at least a stack tonight," Porsche added from the back seat, in her exotic, red bikini outfit.

The three fine females were all light brown, with butts that were super round. Beautiful faces, with no waist. The hot city of Atlanta would surely pay at the Blood Club tonight!

The club sat on Candler Rd, in Greater Decatur, GA. The girls got off on Exit 69, and China Doll pulled into the red-painted, pavement driveway of the all black strip club.

"Boo!" Hammer Head yelled, scaring the stripper heels, hairspray, perfume hell out of the three cuties!

Pow!

Kenya shot him.

"Now, boo that, sucker duck!" Kenya said, laughing in her bikini outfit.

The ladies walked into the club, up the black steps, like divas!

ATL Bad Girls!

"What's poppin'?" Skooter, the seven-foot, three-hundred pound bouncer asked.

He had the biggest muscles and the meanest stare on Earth! Skooter could stare at a hundred hungry lions and make them run!

How in the bull frog heaven ever, he had on a too small, tight, pink tank top. Plus some tight, butt-hugging, plastic-looking, shiny, red leather pants.

'Don't, stop . . . . Pop dat . . .' blasted in the club.

"Yea, that's right! It's make it rain night in Pimp City tonight, baby! If you got funny money, you lame as a Easter bunny. So, if you can't show the finest females in the world no love tonight by tipping, and if you can't buy no drinks from these fine bartenders, because yo baby momma got you on child support, and your project rent is due, Buddy, you ain't gotta go home, but you gotta get the hell outta here! Ha, ha! Throw that money!" D.J. Earl the Pearl yelled from the dark red, tinted D.J. booth.

The entire club was red inside-red chairs, carpet, red pole, and a red stage.

"You want a dance, big boy?" Cheetara asked Pretty Toney.

"You know it! Pop that thang!"

Wap! Toney yelled from his chair, in the back corner of the dark club, next to the red pool table.

Levi, the owner was shooting pool with Dime Piece Daja.

Cheetara smiled, so sexy, adorable, and innocently. She had cheetah paw tattoos from her toes, all the way up her right leg, leading to her cat.

"Muwah!" The pretty, red boy, Tony, who had hazel eyes and curly hair, kissed Cheetara's tat on the bottom of her back, as she bent over and danced in his face.

He was rocket launcher hard. She bounced like a ping pong ball. Fast and hard, to the hypnotizing beat. Dropping that juicy booty on his lap.

Bam!

Then, she turned around, smiled, and sat in his lap.

"Nice tits. Muwah." He tongue kissed her nipples.

She moaned, closed her eyes and . . .

"Ahhhh! Ahh! Freak! Freak hoe! Get this crazy, hungry, stripping slut! Help! She biting my neck! Heeeeelp! Hot sauce hell! Get her! MOMMA!" Pretty Toney yelled.

No one heard a word! The music was much too loud!

Cheetara had a mouth full of live blood. She sat on his lap, with her back turned towards the club. His legs dangled and kicked. She sucked him dry. No one saw him in the corner. His body went limp. He was dead as a star fish in the ocean in 1920!

"One-hundred racks!" Cheetara said, counting the money she took out of the dead man's skinny jeans.

WOOSH!

A black bat flew past her ear! She ducked, and swatted at it with her long fingernails.

Kah Boon! Poof!

The bat turned into a man.

"I got him," Levi, the owner of the club said. Then he carried the body to the basement.

The basement had over five-thousand dead bodies, two-thousand new Nikes, fresh clothes, two million dollars' worth of dead, ex-ballers' jewelry. Famous people, athletes, drug dealers, cheating husbands, doctors, lawyers and all!

Blood Raw Strip Club made two million dollars a week. Once you walked in after midnight, you didn't walk out!

It was 12:01 AM.

"Man . . . something strange about that booty club," fine, female Officer Walker said.

"True. Let's go check it out," the brown-skinned, super-fine Officer Yorker said.

They parked their DeKalb County police cars and walked in . . .

'Damn, I Love a Stripper' by 2 Chains and Nicki Minaj bumped from the red-colored club.

"What in the hell . . ." the officers said in unison, the gummy bear second they walked in.

Reverend Brown stopped his salvation, white on white Corvette.

"Lord, forgive me. I have to go in here and check this out. Stay in the car, Saniya, Asia and Destiny," he told his girls.

Reverend Brown had on a five-hundred thousand dollar, all red, Versace suit, and a red tie to match.

"Good God!" Rev said the snicker bar second he walked in.

"Boy, take off that pink. It's a sin to be that stupid," Reverend Brown told the huge guy in pink.

"AHHHHHH!" he yelled...

"Want a drink, sir?" Cute Courtney, the brown, beautiful bartender asked the pastor, wearing her sexy, black bikini set that exposed her bulging, banging breasts. She had a blue-colored, alcoholic drink between her manicured fingernails.

"AHHHHHHHH!" he yelled...

Cute Courtney dropped the drink.

Woosh!

Ciara the stripper, turned into a light-skinned bat!

"Noooooo!" Erica yelled, after she pimp slapped the vitamins out of Bushwick's mouth, for touching her voluptuous, juicy, soft, St. Louis butt!

She bit him.

"Heeeeelp! Hot Wing Vonda! Lick Me Lisa!" Bushwick yelled, when Erica leaped off the stage, and dived on him, biting deep into his throat.

No one paid them any attention. It actually looked like part of her act! Everyone clapped!

Round of applause...

It looked like the short, West-side Bushwick was just carrying her.

Bemm!

They hit the floor.

Erica was on top of him. Her hands were wrapped tightly around her victim's neck.

'Bands To Make Her Dance' blasted as D.J. Earl the Pearl crunk it up.

His teeth grew out! His platinum turned fire-red as he danced and mixed. Fire seemed to be coming off of his all-red Atlanta Falcon's jersey.

"Have a drink, baby?" Veronica, the model, sexy, slim bartender said to the female cops.

Zip!

They instantly locked their eyes on her.

"What in the blue, mother sucker, Long Island Ice Tea, Corona, couchie hell is wrong, cute cops?" Tamala, the sexy, stupid-thick, main, white bartender asked the two pretty, stone-faced ladies, as they sat on the red stools, in their skin-tight uniforms.

"I'm gucci," Officer Yorker said, in her south Georgia accent.

"I'm . . ." Officer Walker started.

"RRRAH!" Tamala yelled as her teeth grew longer than a red ink pen.

She had a stupid, big, black girl booty, and a nice, Florida tan.

Now, she was red as the devil, and had three horns in her head!

She dove over the counter . . .

Pow!

The cute, bow-legged, fine cops fired their guns at the same dang time!

'Now that's the stuff I don't like' blasted from the speakers. D.J. Earl the Pearl got hyper and redder! The entire D.J. booth was on fire and filled with red, female butts, as D.J. Earl the Pearl mixed the down south, strip club music.

Bite! Bite! Gunshot.

Boom. Boom. Boom. Bang. Crack.

Levi, the owner cracked Santana over the head with a red pool stick, for hard gripping his sister, Kenya PimpCity Brown, on her naked, soft behind.

Woof! Whip! Bap!

"Bingo!" Porsche yelled.

She threw an eight ball like a silver bullet straight across the entire club, from the rest room, and knocked out all of Santana's teeth!

"That's my cousin, sucker!" Porsche barked.

Whif! Woof! Whim!

She turned into a red-boned, big booty, sexy, stripper bat, then flew across the club, and ate him up, up, up, up, up, as the song, 'Ima Beast That Couchie up, up, up, up, up,' blasted out the speakers.

"Calm down, cousin!" D.J. Earl the Pearl yelled from the D.J. booth to Porsche, and continued to dance!

D.J. Earl the Pearl had red eyes, red, short, super wavy hair, and red, vampire-razor, sharp, gold teeth!

POW!

D.J. Earl the Pearl shot E.P., the East Point, couchie tricking client in the head, instantly, with his red, vampire 44 Magnum. The bullet went straight through the red, fiber-glass, D.J. window. However, in the vampire, ghetto world, the hole closed up, instantly, after the bullet went through.

D.J. Earl remembered when E.P. snuck up behind his brother Pimp City in Valdosta State Prison, and stuck him in the neck, with five more people. Pimp City, the vampire, took E.P.'s knife, and stuck it up his rump! He never touched the ground, after fighting all five of the niggas like a vampire-fighting, thugged-out pimp! D.J. Earl still killed E.P., smack in the middle of the club.

Woosh!

E.P.'s small glass of gin flew in the air.

Zip! Zip! Swallow!

The Jamaican, fire, brown-skinned bat flew through the air, and drank the gin butt naked in the air!

The bat flew on stage and whip! The bat hit the top of the red stripper pole and boom! The bat hit the bottom of the red stage and her booty grew out and started clapping!

Danie was Jamaican hot! Danie was one fine, hot, Jamaican, vampire stripper!

The judge and two profession basketball players walked in, then a billionaire, black, swagged-out, hood author walked in the club.

All four gentlemen had at least one-hundred thousand ones to throw!

"AHHHHHH!" Danika, the sexy Seattle/North Carolina stripper yelled, as she bumped into the V.I.P. red sofa.

Danika was too pretty. She pulled out a red sword on the four-hundred pound judge, as he sat on the couch, as his horny, hungry, country, crooked-law, biscuit-chewing, juicy fruit, bad snake booty breath, perverted behind sat on the sofa smiling, with his eyes closed.

Danika sat on his lap with the sword.

SWOOP!

She chopped off his head!

"Yea, sucker!" Kenyatta yelled at the lawyer. Then the Chicago/ Champaign, IL vampire, cutie ripped his penis off, and slung it slap out of the ceiling of the club! It landed on the moon!

"Yeah, yeah! One o'clock! The party is just gettin' crunk!" D.J. Earl the Pearl yelled.

"Help! Lawd! Good, Lawd!" Alonzo and Doug yelled.

"Don't be scared now," Ivory smiled.

Chop ... Chop ...

"Give me a bite, sis," Debra, the pretty dancer said, laughing with a Sprite in her hand.

CHAPTER 2
THE FREAKS COME
OUT AT NIGHT

Outside ... ZOOM!

Miss Weaver sped down the notorious Glenwood Rd., made famous by East Atlanta rappers, For Glenwood Day.

Crystal was smoking hot, as a fire cracker on the 4th of July, in China! Crystal had on all red, and was on a red motorcycle with platinum gas pedals. She was dark as chocolate; pretty as a beautiful queen; finer than a stripper with no waist, and a booty you would pay to have!

"Dang!" Crystal complained.

There was a road block at the red light of Columbia and Glenwood.

"Mam, can I see your driver's license?" the short, butt-naked, nappy headed officer asked.

"Ahhh! This chick biting me!" he screamed like a pissy, hungry, sick baby.

Two female officers raced to his rescue, attempting to save their fellow comrade! Officer Cedra and Officer Shanecia!

"That's on my twin! I don't play that!" the sexy officer, Shanecia shouted with her gun aimed at Crystal.

"Drop the cop!" cute officer, Cedra ordered.

Bump! Bloop!

Crystal dropped the cop.

"What's your problem? Freeze and don't move; or I'll blow your head to the middle of moon," Officer Shanecia said, gun still aimed at Crystal's pretty, natural, curly head.

ZOOM. Screeeach!

The supervisor, Las Vegas, now Decatur cop, Dreauna pulled up. She jumped out of the car, with a ten inch, red, shot gun aimed at Crystal, the suspect.

Dreauna was furiously hot about her wounded officer. She called for backup.

"Hey, I give up. Stop pointing them guns at me," Crystal said, with both hands in the air.

ZOOOSH!

YANK! YANK!

Out of nowhere, Vampire, D.J. Earl the Pearl flew down, scooped her up, and flew her to the strip club!

"Daaaaaang . . ." all the cops and innocent bystanders said, amazed.

"Wow, Aunty Jaz, Ima write that in my autobiography," eight year old, Saniya said as she, Jasmine, Jameka, Sook, and Trapp sat at the light in the candy apple, red Cadillac truck.

Pow. Pow. Pow . . .

Officer Hot Sauce Jackson fired into the air.

"What?! Don't just stand there! Cedra, Shanecia, Dreauna, do something!" the mean, hamburger chin, cock-eyed Lt ordered.

"Ok."

Zip! Zip! Away!

The three girls turned into blue, vampire, police bats, and flew after the suspect! They pursued them to the Blood Raw Strip Club, landed, and ran into the club.

"Freeze!" the girls yelled.

"Ha, ha. Just playing. Let me get a drink," Officer Cedra said to the sexy, hot stripper, Stozzi.

The cops tucked their weapons, and sat at the bar.

"What?!" Stozzi yelled at the cops.

"Ahhhhh!" they screamed.

to be continued . . . .

EXCERPT FROM
LOVE AND FOOTBALL
BY JOSHUA LEVI BROWN

CHAPTER 1
LOVE RULES ALL

'I Will Always Love You...'

Whitney, one of the greatest voices ever known to the human race. She sang loud, pleasant, and beautifully from the four speakers in my bedroom.

I lay on my back, as she lay, peacefully on my ripped, muscular, tatted-up chest.

I love my girl. No lie. No games. Straight up. Real talk, in Real Life Action. I got her back.

I ain't never doing her wrong. Never going to cheat. Never going to hit her or leave her side.

We were the perfect couple!

Match made in heaven! Bam!

High school superstars! She was the prettiest, most-popular cheerleader, and I was the all-star quarterback.

Now, she was rested in my arms. She was so beautiful. I'm just happy man, looking at her sleep like a baby.

"I love you," Ebony mumbled, reading my mind, while she continued to sleep.

"I love you too," I said, smiling, while running my fingers through her long, curly, Indian and black, natural, pretty hair.

Dang! Her body was banging! Her butt looked like a juicy fruit mixed with a basketball!!! Sticking, well, poking out. Round and perfect. Even from underneath our red, silk sheets.

Ebony's body was cold as ice! Rich like gold! Fine as wine! Priceless, like a diamond! Delicious like ice-cream! Sweet as a Georgia peach!

She had caramel, smooth-as-silk skin to set off her slim waist and pretty face!

Ebony was top model tall at 5'10". Then, she was funny, loyal, and athletic at the same dang time! Gymnastic moves, video vixen booty, hypnotizing, hazel eyes, and cheerleader energy like WOW!

Ebony was the love of my life. Of course, I'm a brown-skinned, hard-core, pretty boy with a gangstafied attitude. Lol.

Pow! Pow! Boom! Boom! Boom!

"God!"

Gunshots erupted from every direction. Bullets ripped through the windows and walls in my bedroom.

Instantly, I grabbed my queen, and shielded her body. I lay on top of her, covering her body completely.

Glass shattered everywhere! My heart beat faster than a drunk driver in a race car!

Boom!

Someone kicked the door open . . .

Thump . . .

I rolled our bodies off my king-sized water bed and rolled us underneath the bed.

"Who shooting, baby? What's da—"

"Shhhhush baby. Quiet," I whispered to my trembling, terrified queen. I held her body tight and close to my heart, like a pacemaker.

The room was solid black . . .

"You will die! You and your pretty, innocent, cheer-leading girlfriend! You may be a NFL star quarterback, but you still have dues to pay. You violated the Blood gang. No need to hide under the bed."

Click . . .

The lights came on. I peeked from under the bed. Three killers. They had on red shoes, black clothes, red ski masks, and red, evil-glowing eyes!

Sniffling. Crying. Trembling. Body vibration.

My girl was shaking with fear. The fear of dying an early, young death. Who wants to die? We can't die. God. Not like this!

A week before the Super bowl. Atlanta is picked to win, by ten. I'm the rookie of the year! Plus, the first, black, starting quarterback ever, picked to win the Super bowl, by Vegas, in history!

Now, my high school sweetheart was about to be murdered with me, in my arms. Because of my mistake . . .

Boom!

"Cim! Cim!"

"Huh? Hu . . . Huh?" I stuttered, drooled and jerked.

"Wake up, baby! You had a nightmare! You are sweating like a Friday night slut! I know you got the biggest game on Earth coming up, Sunday. The Super bowl is gigantic! Everybody knows that, baby. But stop sweating. Relax. You made it this far, you will win. Believe me, baby. God is with you," Ebony told me.

She was so confident, positive and sure. She was always my motivation. Ebony believed God gave us the natural ability to accomplish anything. Period.

"Ouch. What da?" I quickly snatched the silk sheet off me and looked at my right leg. Dang, Mary Jane, Cain and Zayne!

A red, fire ant bit the living hot sauce pain out of me!

Hold up . . . A red ant?

Dreaming of red ski masks . . . red shoe . . . where they do that at? Was this a sign? My team wear red and black. That gangstafied, powerful, Atlanta color.

"F—it!! I'm ready! Give daddy a kiss," I told my sexy, sweet love.

Then, I climbed on top of my future wife for life, and we passionately tongue kissed like erupting volcanoes; sexy hot!

CHAPTER 2
WE READY

"Go! Go! Go! Deep! Go deep!" Deon yelled to my star wide receiver, Sergio.

"Bam! Touchdown!" I shouted.

"Yeah, playah! Boop! Boop! I told you, I got that goodle, oodle, noodle, fye game, baby!" Deon joked and bragged.

He was my back-up quarterback. Very talented and quick as the speed of light. He ran 4-2, just like me. We also used Deon to return kicks on the special teams.

Boy, he was so excited to throw a touchdown to Sergio in practice!

He was sticking out his tongue out, doing the Moonwalk.

"Wooh! Oops!"

He fell! The entire team laughed.

"You silly. Get up, De," his twin sister, Shawn, said, as she grabbed his left and right hand to pull him up.

Shawn was one of our forty beautiful cheerleaders. Light-skinned and innocent cute.

"Hey! Huddle up. Motivation. Dedication. Preparation. Determination. This is our game, our shine, our show, our glow. Our game to win. We must not slack. Go hard. No slipping. No turnovers. No mistakes. No doubts. We cannot, and will not, underestimate the underdogs. This is the biggest game on Earth. We live our whole lives to play and win. This game, this is it. One, two, three . . ."

"We ready!" We all shouted simultaneously when coach Joshua Brown finished up his pep speech.

Coach Brown was one of the coolest in the NFL, at 37. He could motivate a pig to score a touchdown! Touchdown Porky the Pig! Lol. Coach Brown made you feel like you could do anything!

The team separated. Practice lasted five, long hours.

"Look, dawg. I want this game. I was born and raised in Atlanta. Forever I love Atlanta. My dreams as a kid was to bring a championship to my city. We need that man, bad!" Sergio told me as we walked out of Pantersville practice field in Decatur, GA.

Sergio was my best friend. He was the top NFL wide receiver, four years in a row. He had fourteen-hundred receiving yards this year.

Super Sergio could catch a bullet with one finger if I threw it!

That boy could catch anything! Plus, he could jump sky high!

I was fresh in the NFL. I took his advice, because he was an experienced vet, and I was an energetic, young rookie.

"What up, nicca?" Micki, a.k.a. Red Bone Shawty, asked me.

I was standing in front of my H-2 Hummer, red and black, of course.

Micki was twenty-one, young, and pretty. She was Coach Brown's feisty, hot girlfriend. You know they met because she my sister. She had that real, red bone attitude, with a little Candler Rd, killa personality. Cause she was humping the best coach in football! You couldn't tell this red chick nothing!

"What it do?" I asked Micki. She swore she ran this team too. Coach Brown was coach of the year, and got a fat eight million dollar contract. Hot damn and ham if Red Bone Shawty ain't blowing every penny!

"Look! Everybody and they momma asking for the hook-up! Give me free Super bowl tickets. Your brother is the quarterback. Blah, blah, blah. My step, great-grand cousin and even my god-cousin want free tickets!" Micki said laughing, but shaking her head.

"Lol. Guuurl, god cousin? Where they do that at? That's a new one," Erica said, smiling. Sexy-chocolate, candy body, cutie. She was my powerful running-back, Levi Bailey's wife. Levi just got a one-hundred and twenty million dollar contract.

Ka-pow!

He was a beast! He once carried five players ten yards on his back, and scored the winning touchdown against Green bay, to get us to the Super bowl!

"That's crazy. Some chick named Ice Bread, a male stripper named Juicy Fruit Johnny and another one named Butt Licking Bobby asked me for free tickets, say they went to school with me girl. Hah, Hah," Ebony, my queen, laughed.

"Guurl. No, they lost they mind, and they foreheads. F—that! I don't care who don't go to the Super bowl. I'm going! V.I.P. baby. That's right! Micki aka Red Bone Shawty, we'll be up through there!" Micki laughed, snapping her fingers.

"True. True. The after party is what's really poppin', anyway!" my baby sister, Pretty Kishana added, with her Cedar Grove High School cheerleading outfit on. She was the only girl at the school with a Benz.

"You're right! We win! Ima tear the city up! Paint the city red, baby! A blunt of loud in one hand, and a bottle in the other, that word to my mother!" Micki added.

"I just want to win. Levi ain't even talking to me right now. He ain't said one word in two weeks! He want to win!" Erica said, crunk.

"Well, I apologize, yall. Everybody can't get a ticket. I did what I could do. I just got to win. We undefeated. So, I want to stay undefeated. Give me a kiss," I told Ebony.

Then, we got into my big boy truck. I drove off, in deep thought. So much intensity. So much hype. So much pressure. All eyes on me. The starter of the biggest game in the world, the Super bowl.

Beyoncé is performing at half-time. My whole family and city is cheering. The whole is world watching. The 2011 Super Bowl was the most watched program in American T.V. history. With an audience of over one-hundred and eleven million viewers. We will top that! So we MUST bring home the Lombardi trophy! I got to win this! I got to, baby! I got to do this for my dad, who got killed last year. He always believed I would do this, even when I had my doubts. I love you, dad. For Ebony, my high school love . . . in Columbia High school, she was the beautiful, brown cheerleader, while I played ball.

In college, at Georgia Tech, we won the national championship. Ebony was a cheerleader. Before each play, right before I got the ball, I would glance over, to see my baby cheering every time.

I love my baby. I love this game.

"Cim?"

"Huh?"

"I'm pregnant . . ."

"What?!"

Screeeeeeach.

I slammed on the brakes.

Bam!

So shocked, I crashed . . . slap, smack into the back of a grey Honda.

I squeezed my baby's hand.

"Are you ok?" I asked her.

Her eyes were as big as a football. Her right hand was covering her mouth. She was a little shook up, like dice.

"Ye, yea . . ." she replied.

Tap. Tap. Tap.

I rolled down my window. It was a mad, Mexican midget. She was adorable, but visibly upset.

"Sir, do you have insurance?" she asked, with a nasty, three-foot tall attitude.

I laughed.

"Insurance? Take this and fix your bumper, baby," I said in a cheerful voice.

When she saw the four-thousand dollars I gave her, she ran faster than a kangaroo on crack!

"Cim, baby. Can you please calm down?"

"Ummm. Yeah, but why you didn't wait till after the Super bowl to tell me?"

"I know. I thought about that. But, now you should have more motivation to win the game. You have to win this for your wife, your family, your fans, your haters, and now, your unborn child."

When those words came out of her mouth, unborn child . . . , I instantly felt a glow. My first born. Cool . . .

"Hello?" I said into my ear phone.

"Someone broke into grandma house!" my little sister, Kishana screamed.

Oh God.

"Ummm. Ima take care of it. Is grandma ok?" I asked.

"No! She is very mad! I'm pissed! Can you come now?"

"I'll be there, Kishana."

What now? My line clicked again.

"Hello?" I asked.

"Hello Cimeon. This is Michael Lackey, the owner of the team. I have a little bad news. The storm from the tornado caused the roof in the dome to collapse. We may have it repaired before Sunday. So let's hope so. The main thing though, let's just win!"

"Sure," I said, shocked.

How much pressure can one man take?

Just win. Just win. Easier said than done. I sat at the next light, pondering about all the extra pressure that just exploded in my lap, a week before the game of my life. What could happen next?

Get hit by a drunk, race car driver? Get pimp-slapped by a skinny elephant? My star running back, Levi, break his arm? I get shot? I mean . . .

Bam!!!

Love and Football . . . .
Coming Soon

A fast-paced, drama-filled book about sports and love.
The passion of the game.
The love of a perfect couple.
The loyalty of a best friend.
The unity of a family.

The shock and steaming pursuit, when his new born baby and fiancé come up missing after the Super bowl . . .

Will he find his new born baby and the love of his life, and still play the game at a high level at the same time? While battling mob members in high places?

Love and Football by Joshua Levi Brown. Next book to come!!!

AFTERWORD- REAL TALK

This is a real life fact, that God said, What Goes Around, Comes Around. Always. Whatever you do in life, will come back to you. Like Erica Bailey said, You do wrong, WRONG WILL DO YOU! You do drugs, DRUGS WILL DO YOU!

Galatians 6:7—A Man REAPS what he sows. If you plant marijuana, you won't grow cocaine! If you plant hate in life, hate will grow on you!

So, my people, live right. Remember, treat people how you want them to treat you. Black men, pick up a pen! You don't have to sin, and fill up the pen! You don't have to trap, rob, rap, or play ball to be rich.

You can pick up a pen. Tell your story. Everybody's got a story to tell. Some say, every gangsta got a story to tell, whatever you think draws your attention.

If you want to be the biggest robber on earth, don't actually do it, just write a book about it!

I wrote these first ten books from prison! Met Erica Bailey, from prison!

God inspired blazing, hot stories out of me-about the streets, even though I've been locked up seven years!

Writing your story, you can be whatever you choose to be! Plus, get rich at the same dang time!

Peace! Challenge yourself!
God Bless!!!
True!!!
Stop Filing up the prisons!
Fill up the book shelves!!!
Truuuue!!!!
Joshua Levi Brown,
The FIGHT writer,
That always, put it down!

Saniya Brown, Joshua's daughter
Smart, story-writing rapper and talented actress. ATL and
Virginia Beach.

Bre'Shauna Cliff
Reppin' Decatur, IL. Young, gifted singer, artist,
dancer, and cheerleader.

Shawn Riley
Actress, model and sister. Reppin' ATL-College Park's Finest

Deon Riley
Super Cool lil' brother and talented rapper-reppin'
West Atlanta and College Park, GA

Porsche Ford
Runway Model, Cover Girl, ATL and Cobb County

Kenya Boyd a.k.a Kenya PimpCity Brown
ATL star, and fashion designer. Reppin' the entire city of Atlanta, GA!

Jasia Shaw a.k.a Sexy Sassy
Actress and Top Model. Vegas Born and Macon, GA raised

Cheetara Smith
Foxy model and Gifted Actress from Columbia High-East
Atlanta and Decatur, GA

Micki Pettis
Cover Girl, actress and business owner. Reppin Decatur's Finest, GA

Cimeon Riley a.k.a Cim R
Versatile New Actor and Star Quarterback in the Upcoming Movie/
Book called <u>Love and Football</u>, reppin' Atlanta and College Park,
GA; and my lil' brother.

Joshua Levi Brown
Author of <u>Real Life Action,</u> and <u>Love and Football</u>.
Reppin' East Atlanta and Decatur, GA.